MAEL

Immortal Highlander, Clan Mag Raith Book 2

HAZEL HUNTER

HH ONLINE

✤

Hazel loves hearing from readers!
You can contact her at the links below.

Website: hazelhunter.com

Facebook:
business.facebook.com/HazelHunterAuthor

Newsletter: HazelHunter.com/news

I send newsletters with details on new releases,
special offers, and other bits of news related to
my writing. You can sign up here!

Chapter One

TEMPTATION, MAEL MAG RAITH realized that morning, made a man wholly dolt-headed.

The unusually warm spring in Scotland had festooned Dun Chaill in flowery vines and ample shade from the flourishing trees. Moss now so thickly carpeted the forest surrounding the castle ruins it had begun creeping up the tumble-down stonework. Daily washed by lavish morning dew, the air smelled like a coddled maiden, soft and sweetly fragrant.

After laboring for weeks to make habitable the intact portion of Dun Chaill's keepe, Mael had quickly agreed to help his chieftain reclaim the kitchen garden. While he had no skill with planting, all of the men had tired of foraging in the sprawling forests. Soon they would need more to add to their limited food sources. The prospect of working outdoors had cheered him as well, for how hard could it prove?

What he should have done, Mael thought as he stood buried to the hips in greenery gone wild, was first have a look at the tangled undergrowth.

"'Tis hopeless, Chieftain," Mael said, grimacing as he pried a spiky thistle from his sleeve. "I say we burn and plant anew."

"You'll tell Jenna she cannae have fresh strewings until the solstice," Domnall mag Raith said as he waded through a white-spangled snarl of hawthorn and meadowsweet. "She ever finds new ways to scatter the sweet herbs for their scents." Standing almost as tall and broad as the tracker, the chieftain looked just as incongruous. "Then bid Edane seek elsewhere wood sorrel for his tonics, and Broden sweet berries for his snares."

"I'd rather beg the Gods smite me." Mael eyed a patch of sky. "Why didnae I remain in the hall to muck out the hearths? 'Tis humble work, and yet can be finished well before the snows arrive. This?" He shook his head.

"'Tis no' so bad. 'Twill need but taming and tending." Domnall surveyed the unculti-vated growth around them. "We should ken the range of what may be saved."

"I'll trodge to the back." Mael peered over a snarled spread of purple blooms before glancing down at the hundreds of pods they'd sprouted. "'Twould seem we willnae want for seed, but I reckon I'd rather eat dirt."

The chieftain grunted. "'Tis good horse fodder, vetch." He reached down and plucked a blushing rose from the undergrowth, a rare smile lighting up his tough features. "We must save some flowers for my lady."

Pushing through the tall grasses until he cleared them, Mael tried to stave off the familiar stab of envy. Since mating with Jenna Cameron, Domnall's nature had vastly changed. He no longer retreated into icy indif-ference and bleak silences. While they all labored in various ways to improve their situa-tion, the chieftain had worked tirelessly to transform the abandoned stronghold. He meant to make it become a true home for his wife and his men. Mael had no doubt that all of it sprang from the deep, abiding love Domnall had found with Jenna.

'Tis their reward for all they've endured, this life they build.

Mael had no illusions about his own future. He'd inherited his defender sire's massive build and outlandish strength, and looked every inch a brute. While some females regarded his size as proof of his virility, none could gaze upon him without a shiver. The lasses of his tribe thought him the same as Fargus mag Raith, who had nightly vented his endless rage on his mate and bairns.

Unlike his sire Mael had always been of a mild, thoughtful temperament. Indeed, he'd often thought it a punishment from the Gods for pairing his cherishing nature with such a fearsome appearance.

Beyond the vetch he found wild carrots and turnips paving the ground with lacy cups and broad fronds of green. The plentiful roots would add flavor to their pottages, and even feed the mounts when grazing grew thin in the cold season. Yet when Mael lifted his gaze he saw they had crept out from under an unkempt hedge of juniper that stretched in an enormous curve that seemed to have no end. Even more puzzling, behind it he could see the top of a wych elm hedge and another of blackthorn growing behind it.

"Chieftain," he called to Domnall as he looked down the long wall of spiky leaves and berries. "We've more than we reckoned back here."

❦

THAT NIGHT when they gathered in the hall for the evening meal, Mael described the tangled area to Jenna Cameron, who nodded.

"I've seen that place," she said as she passed a platter of oatcakes to her mate. "It looks to me like an overgrown hedge maze." She paused as she took in the blank looks the rest of the men were giving her. "That's a garden labyrinth made from shrubs or small trees trimmed to serve as walls. But they date back only as far as the Renaissance—ah, the mid-sixteenth century—so I'm probably wrong."

Mael didn't doubt her, but something

about the carefully planted hedges set his teeth on edge. "And if you're no', lass?"

"'Twas likely meant to catch and end the unwary," said Broden, his handsome face set in its habitual scowl, "like every other facking thing in this place. No matter what 'tis, we should burn it."

Gleaming red braids bobbed as their archer, Edane, nodded. "Aye, spread flames in the midst of all that deadfall and blowdown. We'll clear at least the forest and the ruins before the smoke summons the Sluath to descend on us."

"Let them come." The trapper drove his eating dagger into the top of the trestle table. "We ken how to kill them now."

Kiaran dragged a hand through his red-gold mane, making the kestrel on his shoulder fly off to join the other trained raptors perched in the rafters.

"We're five against a horde of demons," he retorted. "Aye, surely we'll prevail."

"Enough," Domnall said, bringing an end to the argument before it'd begun in earnest. He met Mael's gaze. "As seneschal the grounds as well as the stronghold shall be your domain. What say you?"

Mael was a little startled to be given the position as well as the say, but it seemed sensible. Since boyhood he'd shared the work of his *máthair* and sisters, and had the nature best suited to managing this unruly household.

"'Tisnae a present threat to us," Mael said after giving it more thought. "I'd clear the garden first. Take stock of the maze after, and learn if 'tis safe or no'."

Broden snatched up his food, mumbled something like an apology to Jenna, and stalked out.

Edane made a rude sound, caught Domnall's eye, and then turned his attention to his trencher.

After they finished the meal, Domnall lingered to help Mael bank the hearth and take apart the trestle table. When not in use they hung it on wall hooks.

"I might have first asked you to serve as my seneschal," the chieftain said.

"You never ask, for you're never wrong." Mael grinned at him. "'Tis facking annoying. Dinnae keep your lady waiting so you might smooth my feathers. You plucked them all, long ago."

"Still, Brother." The chieftain inclined his head. "My thanks."

Mael watched him stride off in the direction of the chamber he shared with Jenna. The thought of seeking his own empty bed didn't appeal to him, so he took down a torch. There weren't enough men to stand regular sentry, but he could patrol once around the ruins. It might tire him out, and keep him from staring at the wall cracks for half the night.

Outside the great hall he navigated the warren of dark, cluttered passages from memory until he stepped over the rubble of the inner ward's back wall. Beyond it lay the front of the wild garden. Earlier he and Domnall had cleared a narrow foot trail. As Mael lifted his torch to it for a better view, a sudden, chilly wind blew down it. A distant, booming sound, like echoed thunder seemed to come from the ridges, as well as a strange, stuttering, metallic noise.

Scowling, Mael held the torch higher and surveyed the surroundings. Could the wind have knocked something down? The fluttering torchlight showed only the same overgrown garden and tumbled down stones. A glance at the dark and starless sky revealed nothing as well.

Slowly Mael lowered the torch and decided to take his patrol in the direction of the strange sounds, in the direction of what Jenna had called a hedge maze.

Chapter Two

❧❧❧

THE WIND BUFFETED Rosealise Dashlock with the fervor of an intent to flay her to the bone. Yet even as she whirled and tumbled through the air, she was gladdened. The pale curls lashing her face could be brushed and pinned. Her limbs, now no longer limp and leaden, felt very strong indeed. As soon as she found some footing and a handhold, she would defeat this wretched gale, and then she would...

...and then she would...

There had to be something she would do. Rosealise simply couldn't think of it for the buffeting and twirling.

The clouds below her parted, revealing a

flaring flame, a silhouette of an enormous figure, and a huge web of shadows surrounding both. Instinctively she flipped away from the fire, falling squarely atop the figure beside it, which collapsed beneath her. They both landed with a bone-jarring jolt and a grunt. The fire fell away, illuminating the face of a very large man.

"Such an abominable denouement." She pushed herself up from his very broad chest as his rough shirt grazed her breasts—her bare breasts, she saw as she glanced down. "Hello? Sir? Good gracious, have I killed you?" The large man said nothing, but she rose an inch as he took a breath. "Thank heavens."

Rosealise struggled upright. In addition to straddling the large man in a most inappropriate manner, she hadn't a stitch of clothing on her tall, pale body. She regarded the man's primitive-looking tunic, which she still clutched with both hands.

"Sir, forgive me, but…might I borrow this?"

The man didn't refuse, which satisfied her.

Removing the long shirt required Rosealise

to shift and slide and adjust the poor fellow in an awkward manner. The warmth of his big body kept her from shivering until she could finish disrobing him. He seemed very familiar to her, although she couldn't say why. Black symbols she couldn't read covered the top of his right arm. They seemed most disagreeable to her, until she stood with the removed garment and saw a reflection of the same symbols on her left thigh. When she attempted to rub off the marks they remained, as much part of her skin if she'd been born with them.

"This will not do," she muttered under her breath as she frowned at the black symbols. Surely, she'd never willingly mark herself in such an excessive fashion, if at all. She would hide them from sight until she could acquire some soap and a scrub brush.

The pressing chill of the night air finally prompted her to don the man's long shirt, which fell only to the top of her knees. She arranged the scandalously short length as decently as she could, aware of the decidedly masculine scent he'd left on the rough cloth. He smelled as good as an autumn blaze on a cold night. His garment had been sewn very badly, however, and needed mending in three places.

He must not have a wife to look after him.

She felt oddly gratified by that notion, as well as embraced by his garment. She hugged the rough fabric closer to her. To feel so safe and comforted under such conditions baffled her as much as the shared symbols. Then there was the distinct sense that she knew this man, which only added to her confusion.

Carefully Rosealise knelt beside him, doing her best not to ogle the chest she had bared. Not that it was in any manner lacking of muscle, breadth or width—on the contrary. It seemed to her eyes a map of some exotic, sunwashed land where spices burned in braziers and long dark lashes fringed jewel-bright eyes. His magnificent body also gave off the most sumptuous heated scent, as one might savor on a cold night before a fire of fragrant woods. Such an outlandish fancy seemed new to her, but then she felt sure she'd never beheld a half-naked man.

Egad, but she *was* ogling his chest, quite shamelessly.

"Sir?" Rosealise said as she placed a hand on his bare shoulder, and gave it a gentle shake. "Please do wake up, sir, so I might inquire of you some details. Your name, certainly, and where we are, and how I came to fall here. I daresay I'm not the sort to climb trees or leap from balconies."

Perhaps, if she were very fortunate, he could also enlighten her as to who she was. All she could recall was her name, nothing more.

The man groaned, shuddered, and then opened his eyes. They appeared dark topaz in color, although somewhat unfocused at present. She'd have sworn she knew his face, if she could recall anything from before her unfortunate fall.

Stop being such a gongoozler.

"Good evening." She offered him a prim smile. More friendliness than that might invite unsuitable assumptions and attentions, especially as she sat virtually naked at his side. "My name is Miss Rosealise Dashlock. I'm terribly sorry, but I fear that I dealt you something of a floorer."

The man squinted at her, suggesting that he might not understand.

"I fell atop you and knocked you sense-less," she clarified. "I do apologize, and wish to know to whom I should apologize." Rosealise waited on his reply, but he seemed still dazed. She touched his arm. "You are named…?"

"Mael mag Raith," he said in a deep voice made melodic by a familiar accent. He pushed himself up, tucked in his chin, and then stared at her with such fascination that girlish heat rose into her face.

Such missish behavior would not do.

"Very pleased to make your acquaintance, Mr. mag Raith." Her sense of familiarity in regard to him suggested they had already been introduced in the past, but with her befuddled brain she could not be sure. "If you would tell me how I came to be here?"

His dark brows drew together, and he looked up. "You fell from the sky, lass."

"Yes, that much I do remember." Harrowing as it had been, it seemed less important than the circumstances that had caused her plummet. "Do you know what occurred before my fall?"

"Mayhap." Mael blinked. "I reckon the

Sluath captured and enslaved you from another place—no' America, for you dinnae speak as Jenna—as they did the Mag Raith and our chieftain's lady. You then escaped the underworld by leaping from the demons' sky bridge, which brought you here to Dun Chaill. 'Tis somehow taken your memories from you, as it did Jenna's, and ours."

This flood of astounding particulars quite undid Rosealise, who carefully drew back the hand she'd placed on his shoulder.

"Presumably I jumped from the under- world to this place in an effort to elude the demons who abducted me?" When he nodded, she felt a surge of sympathy. Such a Banbury tale meant the poor man suffered from some form of lunacy, likely aggravated by her dropping on his head. "Well, thank you for that, sir. Perhaps now we should go and find your chieftain."

When Mael rose to his feet Rosealise had to smother a squeak of alarm. The man was simply enormous, like some great statue of a titanic hero brought to life. He held out to her a huge hand.

"Come with me, lass, and stay close. 'Tis likely 'twill want to end us, this maze."

☙❧

MAEL EXPECTED Rosealise to recoil from his touch. When she instead took his hand in a strong, steady grip, he did the flinching. Heat jolted from her palm to his, and spread up his arm like invisible fire. By the time he gathered his reeling thoughts, she had risen to stand in front of him and confounded him anew.

She had so much wayward, curly hair that it hung down to her hips, and gleamed in his torch's light like scrolls of frost. His tunic hung on her tall frame like an over-large sack, but that only emphasized the graceful lines of her long limbs. She had dark gold brows, rosy lips, and a slightly squared chin that balanced the oval of her refined features. Her stature was such that her eyes, of the same silvery gray as dove feathers, looked into his with but a slight tip of her chin.

By the Gods, he'd never seen such a female. She might have been one of the old Eceni's war goddesses, fallen to earth.

"It seems that I am exceptionally long, as you are," Rosealise said, pursing her lips as she eyed her bare feet. She seemed dismayed now. "Happily, far leaner, or your shirt would... well, it's the best we may do."

"I'd give you my trews, but I've naught under... ah..." He looked around them until he saw his tartan flung against the base of a hedge. "Here, lass."

Rosealise watched him shake out the plaid and then stepped back as he held it out to her. "I cannot take your cloak, Mr. Mag Raith. You must be thoroughly chilled by now."

"'Tis hardly cooler than a summer morn, and I'm no' a *maister*. My name 'tis Mael." As he wrapped the violet and black tartan around her shoulders, he breathed in the crisp, clean scent of her, like that of snowfall on a still November morning. As soon as he felt her shiver, he took his hands away. He'd frightened her, likely by telling her too much about the Sluath and her escape. Then he wondered if instead he caused her fright. "You've no more to fear, my lady."

A soft chuckle escaped her. "I am no lady, sir...Mael. I work. I work as... I am..." She frowned and pressed her fingers to her temple. "The headache regrettably prevents my calling to mind my work at present." She squinted at him. "Might we go now?"

That meant walking out of the maze, and be facked if Mael could remember how he'd gotten into it. Dimly he recalled pushing through the outer hedge, and picked up his torch to examine the nearest walls—walls which now had begun sprouting long wooden branches covered in sharp metal thorns.

"Mayhap I spoke too soon." Mael turned his head until he spied the top of Dun Chaill's only intact tower, and then took hold of Rosealise's arm. "This way with me, lass."

"Oh, blazes." She held out her other hand, across which he saw a long, thin scratch oozing blood. "You have exceedingly unpleasant shrubbery here, sir, in dire need of trimming. You should give your gardener the sack."

"I shall burn the place on the morrow," he promised as he hurried her along with him. Ahead of them more of the thorned branches appeared, and began spreading into the gap between the two hedge walls. "Lass, forgive me."

"Forgive you for—oh, my." She flung her arms around his neck a moment after he snatched her up. "Sir, this is most unseemly."

"Aye." He shifted sideways and back again to avoid the stabbing branches, and then spotted his own tracks. "Hold tight now, lass."

Mael looked ahead with his eyes far-seeing and at last spotted the opening in the hedge. It had been somehow hacked out of the juniper, as if he'd done so with his sword, which as he recalled remained inside the great hall where he'd left it.

"May I have that torch a moment?" Rosealise asked, and when he handed it to her, she waved the flames at the branches, which shrank back into the hedges. "Beware now. I see a very large hole in the ground there, by that gap in the greenery. I daresay we shall fall into it should we attempt to leave by that route, sir."

"Mael. Mayhap." He shifted her so that her chest and hips pressed against his. "Put your legs around my waist."

"I've no notion of what you mean."

Rosealise made a shrill sound as he hoisted her thighs around him. "Mael, I cannot believe I'm accustomed to such behavior."

He glanced over his shoulder to see the space behind them filling up with thorny branches. "'Tis a run now, lass, or we shall be skewered."

"As I see. Well, then." She sighed and clutched him tightly. "Onward, my dear sir, onward."

Mael backed up a few steps, hissing as thorns prodded his bare back. He then ran at the gap, waiting until the last possible moment before he jumped. His powerful legs projected them both over the pit-trap and through the juniper, and when he landed, he promptly fell face-down atop Rosealise.

He propped himself on his elbows and looked down at her dazed expression. "So, 'twas like this for you with me, then?"

She closed her eyes for a moment, and he saw the gleam of a tear clinging to her pale lashes. When he used his thumb to brush it away, she took in a deep breath and smiled up at him.

"Thank you, sir. You've saved my life twice now."

It had been so long since Mael had been so close to a female that he didn't want to move. *No, 'tis her. Only and ever her.* That ridiculous thought made him push himself up and off her.

Rosealise swiped her fingers over her cheeks, sniffing as she rose. She then quickly tugged down the edge of his tunic, as if trying to cover as much of her legs as possible.

"If I may be so unmannerly to inquire, what do those marks on your arm signify?"

His jaw tightened as he glanced down at his Sluath tattoo. He hated the strange inked glyphs, but to remove them he'd have to skin himself.

"'Tis a brand, I reckon."

"I'm also marked." She touched her leg. "Mine appear to be the reverse of yours."

Mael thought of Jenna's skinwork, which matched Domnall's. "Mayhap the same fiend marked us both. We're as cattle to the demons."

"Ah, yes. The demons." She turned toward

the wall of the outer ward. "Blazes. Is this a castle?"

Mael nodded. "'Tis Dun Chaill, home now to the Mag Raith. Much in ruins, yet we mean to rebuild it."

"An admirable goal." For a moment sadness flickered across Rosealise's face. "Where in it might we find your chieftain?"

Chapter Three

⚜

BEING ROUSED FROM his bed to greet a strange, half-dressed female had Domnall wondering if he yet dreamed. Jenna, who woke with him, obviously recognized the towering lass as one of the females who escaped the Sluath with them. She said nothing as Mael introduced Rosealise Dashlock, and then ushered her into their chamber.

"I regret I must disturb you both at this wretched hour," Rosealise said. "But Mael has related a tale of my escaping an underworld that seems quite, ah, fantastic."

The sound of her voice echoed through Domnall's thoughts, familiar and warming, as if a pleasing song. From that recollection came a single word, uttered in his own voice: *Dash.*

"I'll explain to Miss Dashlock what's happened," Jenna said. "You two should go build up the fires and put on a brew." She handed Mael one of her mate's tunics. When neither of them moved she added, "The lady needs to dress, guys."

On their way to the great hall Mael related the details of his encounter with Rosealise in the maze. That she had plummeted out of the sky and retained no memory of her past life made it obvious that she had been a Sluath slave. Jenna had found her way to them in the same manner.

"I told her more than I should, Chieftain," his tracker admitted as they retrieved some logs from the woodpile the men had stacked in the corner of the hall. "'Twas unnerving, to see her there in my tunic, looking the goddess with her hair loose about her. 'Twas so addling I forgot to guard my tongue. Now she reckons me crazed."

"Jenna shall assure her you're no'." He watched Mael struggle into his tunic. "The goddess fell *naked* from the sky, then."

"Aye. I thought you larger." He rolled his shoulders against the too-tight seams before he caught Domnall's gaze. "Dinnae smirk at me. 'Twas no' as if I summoned a female in the scud to drop on my head."

"Never should I reckon different." But he heard the softer shift in Mael's tone whenever he spoke of Rosealise, and the new worry in his eyes. "Ken you the lady from our time in the underworld?"

"I recall naught of her or that," Mael admitted. He looked as if he might say more, and then rubbed his brow. "I'll go see to a brew."

Jenna came to the hall with Rosealise a short time later, and smiled at Domnall as she led the woman to sit by the now blazing hearth. It amused him to see his spare tunic, trews and boots fit the tall blonde's length, if not her much-thinner frame and smaller feet.

"I daresay I've never donned pantaloons or bloomers," Rosealise said as she sat down and regarded his trews. "Quite comfortable and practical. Doubtless why men never allow us to wear them." She looked up at Domnall. "As soon as I may secure more suitable attire, Chieftain, I will launder and return yours."

"'Tis of no concern." He walked over to stand beside the heavy wood mantle so that he faced both women. "My wife spoke to you of how and why we came here?"

"She did explain, most thoroughly," Rosealise said, her expression shifting to remorse. "I regret that I briefly regarded Mael as a lunatic." She looked around them. "I should like very much to apologize to him for my mistake."

The softness in her tone suggested she wanted to do more than that, which pleased Domnall. Of all his hunters, Mael had been unwavering in his loyalty to the Mag Raith. As a man devoted to his family, he'd also suffered the most from the loss of their tribe and their solitary, outcast existence among the druids. A tall, strong lady like Rosealise might make him the perfect mate.

"Mael is preparing a brew, something like tea," Jenna said to her, and then met his gaze. "I do remember saying goodbye to Miss Dashlock in the underworld, and she has a

Sluath tattoo, so she was definitely imprisoned there with us. The reason she sounds different from me is that she's English." His wife glanced at the other woman. "You have a vaccination scar on your arm. Do you know when you got that?"

"Horrid sickness, small pox. I...oh." Rosealise uttered a small sound of dismay and rubbed the back of her neck. "Do you know, I suffer the most dreadful ache in my head whenever I try to recollect even the smallest detail of my life?"

"It's the same for me," Jenna said. "Unlike us, Domnall and his men remember their past without any difficulty. They were hunters before the Sluath captured them."

Domnall guessed why his wife was choosing her words so carefully. She had not yet informed Rosealise that she had travelled through time, or that Jenna and the Mag Raith were immortals.

"Now we're become builders, and Jenna our architect," Mael said, his tone deliberately hearty as he emerged from the kitchens with a tray of steaming mugs, oatcakes and fruit. "If

you'll take charge of this, my lady?" he said to
Jenna as he handed her the tray.

Domnall went to help him set up the
trestle table, watching his gaze as it kept
straying back to Rosealise. "What think you?"

"She's an iron wildflower," Mael promptly
answered. "Such beauty, and yet so sure and
strong." He looked intently into Domnall's
face and glowered in return. "I but admire her
courage, as I've done Jenna's."

"You've never looked at my wife thus," he
told him, "or I'd have put you on your arse."

Dawn arrived soon as they assembled the
table, and the other Mag Raith emerged from
their chambers. Each stopped to stare at
Rosealise before moving to join Domnall and
Mael. In a low voice the chieftain quickly
related what had happened before asking the
ladies to come to the table.

After introductions to the other men
Rosealise sat beside Jenna and inspected them
openly, earning a smile from Edane and a
narrow look from Kiaran. Broden seemed to
be looking anywhere but at the
Englishwoman.

"You chaps seem a quite capable lot," Rosealise said, her tone briskly pleasant. "I've no doubt you're the reason we ladies escaped the underworld. For my part I do thank you. Have any of you written to your families to make them aware of your adventures?"

Before anyone spoke Broden said, "We cannae write, and we've no living kin. 'Tis just the five of us, and our chieftain's wife." He seemed oblivious to Mael's glower, his rasping voice grew soft as he asked, "Ken you any of us, my lady?"

Rosealise took a moment to carefully study each face again before she sighed. "I'm afraid I don't recognize anyone, sir, although Mael seems somewhat familiar to me. Jenna tells me in time my memories may return, so if we were acquainted, I pray my ignorance of it only temporary." She eyed the tracker for a moment, and her lips curved.

Broden nodded, but Domnall had the odd sense that he was angry.

"What shall you do now, my lady?" Kiaran asked.

"You've all been exceedingly kind to me,

and I'm so grateful," the Englishwoman said
briskly. "Yet I feel I should seek lodging elsewhere until I may regain some inkling of my
personal situation. Perhaps there is an inn in a
nearby village?" Before someone answered she
touched her brow. "I forget, I have no money
to pay for rooms, or memory of family or
friends who might assist me. It seems I must
trespass on your hospitality a little longer,
Chieftain."

"Think naught of it," Domnall told her.
He had no intention of allowing her to leave
Dun Chaill, but if she thought that her own
idea, all the better.

"Well, then that's settled." Rosealise
glanced at one of the tree trunks supporting
the boughs and thatch they'd installed as a
roof over the hall. "This is admirable work
you've done here. I'm quite impressed by the
clever manner by which you've preserved
nature's additions to this room. Do you
imagine the trees will continue to grow?"

As Jenna described how the men had first
topped the trees and stripped their branches
before building the roof, Broden rose from his
seat. He caught Domnall's eye and gave a tilt

of his head before he retreated into the kitchen. The chieftain followed, and found his trapper adding water to the brew pot.

"We shallnae frighten her, if 'tis your worry," he told Broden, and watched him toss a handful of herbs and spice to the water. "As we learned with Jenna, 'tis better to measure out truth in small portions."

"'Tis no' that." The trapper glanced out into the hall before he said in a lower voice, "Since we came here, I've been dreaming of a lass. I cannae recall her features, but her long, pale hair, aye. 'Twas the same as the lady's. 'Twere no such females among our tribe, so I ken I met her in the underworld."

Domnall frowned. "Why didnae you say?"

"In my dreams the lass shares my bed." His jaw tightened. "Naked, as we kiss and touch. Although I ken no more than that, doubtless we facked."

"Jenna said 'twere other females who escaped with us." He thought of Mael's besotted looks at the Englishwoman and rubbed his brow. "You cannae tell her, Brother."

"Think you I would?" Broden rose and

bunched his fists. "I ken that I'm slave-born, and lower than swine. You neednae remind me."

Before Domnall could explain his meaning the trapper stalked out.

Chapter Four

✤

IN THE FIRST light of dawn Galan
Aedth sat in the center of a midland
glen and silently fumed. The last of his
channeling crystals sat on the stele before him,
flickering like a rushlight in a breeze. His
chilled hands felt none of its power as he tried
again to draw from it. To see the faint
glimmer of magic wink out confirmed his
suspicions.

Useless.

Galan rose from the spell circle, leaving
behind the crystal and the stele as he made his
way through the tall grass to his mount.
Despite his efforts to conserve his power it had
slowly drained away over the last weeks. The
charms he carried would maintain his protec-

tive body ward for only a few more hours. Without more power to recharge them he was as useless as a mortal.

For this quest Galan had sacrificed much. Thanks to the Mag Raith and Jenna Cameron he'd lost his position as headman of the Moss Dapple, and had been banished from his tribe. He had no wish to return to the enchanted forest, even to dwell among his own kind, so that was of little consequence. What burned in him was the need for vengeance against the Pritani and their hoor. His pursuit of them had forced him to bargain with the Sluath. The soul-stealing demons had proven even more terrifying than the old legends had claimed. Yet they had also promised him in return for the Mag Raith the one dream denied him for centuries.

Fiana, his dead mortal wife, would be returned to him, unless he failed to give the demons what they wanted.

He stopped and crouched to remove the horse's hobble when another disagreeable thought occurred to him. The gods saw to it that druid kind could return to the mortal realm from the well of stars. When Galan died his next death, he would not reincarnate again.

He straightened, and gripped the carved shell pendant hanging from his neck. In hopes of gaining the secret of immortality he had deceived the Mag Raith into serving him for twelve centuries. He'd wanted eternal life so that he might have time to discover how his mortal wife might reincarnate as druids did. By abandoning him, the wretched Pritani had condemned Galan to the same fate as his beloved Fiana.

If I fail, I shall die and like her be lost forever.

Galan knew he had set himself upon the dark path ever since learning that the Sluath were more than superstitious legends. All the warnings he'd ignored over his many lifetimes now would come true. He'd squandered his power and his soul for a love he'd never again know, and an existence ever denied his kind. Another druid might have felt regret and shame.

His rage fed on the humiliation to burn ever higher.

A shadow blocked the rising sun, and Galan saw the fringe of the dark gray clouds racing toward him. Strange flashes of light within the fast-moving storm made him force his legs to walk toward it. The lightning that sliced down to strike the glen made clots of dirt and grass fly into the air as he stood and watched. The light flashes spread, grew brighter, and took on form.

Winged men, godlike and arresting in beauty, flew down to land before him. Each had a beguiling form, and the vision they presented seemed that of a celestial gift being bestowed. Their immense wings flared out before folding and disappearing into their backs. Magic shimmered over them, transforming the demons into seemingly ordinary mortal men. Only one did not change, but strode up to Galan in all his white-gold glory.

"Tree-worshipping scum," muttered Prince Iolar as he tried to punch through Galan's body ward. He snarled with rage as his efforts only produced a spray of hot sparks. "You cursed dirt crawlers murdered my scout. Was it your doing?" His golden eyes narrowed. "Did you betray my trust?"

"Never, my prince." Galan went down on one knee, and kept his head bowed low. It shocked him to hear that the demons could be killed, for they had always seemed utterly omnipotent. But if it had happened, he could conceive of only one band who might have accomplished it. It also occurred to him that he could immediately turn such knowledge to his advantage. "'Twas the Mag Raith that killed your man, I'm sure of it. They ken much of you and your kind from their time in the underworld. 'Tis the only reason they escaped."

Iolar uttered a vile curse and walked away from him.

Galan slowly rose. "I shall take your scout's place, if I may, my prince."

Some of the demons chortled as the prince glared at him. "Have you forgotten that you're mortal and bound to the dirt, you idiot?"

"No, my prince." Telling them he no longer belonged to druid kind seemed the swiftest way to a bad end. "You've magnificent power, capable of such great transformation and magic. 'Twould be naught for you to give me the ability to fly, and such powers as I need to carry out your orders."

Iolar tilted his head to peer at him as if he'd sprouted another eye. "You want to become like us?"

"I couldnae aspire to such eminence as you possess," Galan said quickly. "But with wings, and more power, I'd better serve you and your aims."

The prince walked around him. "You will have to lower your wards for me to transform you." He stopped in front of him and bared his teeth. "Have you the spine to do that, Aedth?"

"If it needs be done, aye." He could feel his body ward beginning to wane even now, so he had no choice but to take the risk. "'Twill serve as proof of my loyalty to you, my prince."

Galan removed the warding charms from his garments, and hurled them away. He then spread his arms and bowed his head, filled with such fear that bile flooded his mouth.

Iolar reached out to press his claws against his tunic, and then used them to rip the garment off. Sweat ran down Galan's face as he waited for the Sluath to ram his hand into his chest, but remained unmoving. He knew the fear of death then, as he never had before, yet life meant nothing to him without Fiana.

"So, you do mean to serve me. Or perhaps yourself, but no matter." The prince moved to stand at his back. "Danar, Seabhag. Hold him." Against Galan's ear he murmured, "Agony as you have never known awaits, Druid. Be a good boy and endure it."

The two Sluath came to flank him, and gripped his arms cruelly tight. Galan jerked as the prince's icy claws tore down the flesh of his back, which he imagined to be the worst of it, until the Sluath rammed sharp stakes into the open wounds over and over. Galan emptied his belly on the ground before he gathered in enough breath to scream.

"Do something about the noise, Seabhag," Iolar said before impaling Galan again.

The shifting demon stuffed something foul into his mouth, cutting off Galan's air and voice. Yet the torture continued, on and on until a frozen blackness crowded into his head. It came from the wounds, which were puckering around the stakes protruding from them.

When the two demons released him, he collapsed, his body wracked by such pain that he curled over, knowing that only his beloved could be worth such suffering.

"Rise, Aedth." The prince came to stand before him, his claws and wings dripping with blood. "Let me see if the change has taken."

Somehow Galan staggered to his feet, and flinched as Iolar slapped his hand against his chest. The chill that spread through him from the touch numbed the pain, however, and when he opened his eyes, his body filled with strange power.

"You bear the feathers of our prince on your back," Meirneal said, sounding petulant and envious. "Show your gratitude for his gifts."

Galan moved his shoulders, and great wings fanned out on either side of him. When he turned his head, he saw them, snowy white and scarlet red.

"You remain mortal, but only just," Iolar told him. "It will take a day or two before you fully heal, but when you do my feathers will allow you to fly, and with my power you may cast your spells." He cradled Galan's chin in his claws, smearing him with his own blood.

"Betray me, Aedth, and this will seem a brief and loving caress."

"Never, my prince." With some difficulty he folded his wings, bowed, and uttered the first real lie he'd ever told Iolar. "My thanks."

Chapter Five

❧❧❧

ROSEALISE COULD CLEARLY see that adapting to the rustic conditions inside the castle would prove a trial. As Jenna showed her around the keepe for the first time, the other woman seemed not to notice. But Dun Chaill had fallen to ruin ages ago, judging by the pervasive disorder and decay. Enormous trees grew in the most inconvenient spots. Moss greened the ashlar, and the leaf rot and detritus of centuries carpeted every floor and flat spot. What she wouldn't give for a decent broom and a dozen young housemaids with strong backs.

"You mentioned that Mael is in charge of

the household," she said to Jenna as they skirted a bed of fern sprouting from some rotted floor timbers. "Why hasn't he hired staff to help with the restoration?"

"We don't have any money for that, and we'd rather keep the place to ourselves for now." The younger woman sounded as if she were choosing her words carefully. "Domnall and his men tend to be very independent."

Aside from the great hall, and some of the surrounding chambers, nothing appeared to have proper roofing. Gaps in the stonework allowed both chill and wind to disperse what heat came from the fireplaces, some of which she suspected had chimneys in need of a thorough sweeping. The absence of furnishings and drapery completed the dismally hollow tableau.

"We haven't made much progress with the interior yet," Jenna said. "As an architect I understand design and theory, but I have no practical experience at building and renovations. Neither do Domnall and his men, so it's a lot of trial and error."

"One of the gentlemen seemed quite different from the others," Rosealise said, and reached to brush a leaf from the other woman's shoulder. "Edane, I believe his name was."

"Our archer." Jenna said and nodded. "What he lacks in bulk he makes up for with accuracy with his bow. I've never seen him once miss a target. He was in training to become a shaman, a tribal healer," she added quickly. "He knows a lot about herbs and plants, which I don't, so that's handy. He just hates… Oh, here's your room."

Rosealise stopped with her in front of a newly-made door.

"The castle's main pantry is at the end of the passage, and that opens out into the garden and the kitchens, so we think these were servants' quarters. We're still working on the basic necessities," Jenna said as she opened the door into a small chamber. "But at least you won't have to sleep out in the hall."

Rosealise peered in at the lumpy, fur-draped wooden pallet, bare stone walls and cold hearth. Ends of greenery protruded from the edges of the low bed. A tiny window slit provided some air but very little light. She could feel the damp from where she stood at the threshold.

A sense of having occupied many other such small, uninviting rooms came over her. Had she been too poor to acquire better? But wondering that sent a sharp ache through her head, so she turned her attention to the room again, and what she might do to enhance it.

"It should be very cozy," she said and glanced down the corridor at the other chambers. "Do the rest of you keep rooms here?"

"Domnall and I are using the winery on the other side of the tower for our quarters," Jenna told her, "and Edane and Kiaran are sharing the old granary beyond the opposite tower. But Mael and Broden are just down the hall if you need anything."

Knowing the strapping hunter slept so close sent Rosealise's emotions into a churn. She felt safest whenever he was near, and yet also somewhat undone. She didn't feel familiar with being dependent on anyone, indeed quite the opposite, but his proximity made her insides pleasantly warm.

Noticing Jenna's regard, she said, "Once

I've lit the fire and collect some proper ticking for the mattress, I will be quite content."

"We don't have the materials to make real bedding yet," the other woman admitted. "For the moment we're using evergreen boughs under what sacking and furs we have." She wrinkled her nose. "I've tried to think of a better solution, but I'm not much of a housekeeper."

"Nonsense. You've done well for a lady alone in a household of gentlemen." She thought for a moment. "I believe I saw a great, grassy clearing through one of the front wall gaps. Cut, dried and bundled properly, the grass should serve better as ticking, or fleece perhaps. By chance do you have sheep?"

Jenna shook her head. "There are some villagers who herd theirs at the far end of the valley, but we have to be careful about approaching them. They're not thrilled about us living at Dun Chaill. They believe a monster rips apart anyone who comes near here."

"You're certainly proof there is no such thing, although your garden is rather beastly."

She touched the other woman's arm. "Considering all the dangers you've encountered, it seems very odd that you'd choose such a place to inhabit. Is the reason to do with the other matters that you and the chieftain have decided to conceal from me?"

"Yes," the younger woman said and winced. "I didn't mean to— You're very perceptive."

"Yet not so easily shocked, I daresay." She smiled. "Don't fret, my dear. I'm a stranger to you all, and that is reason enough to withhold your confidences. I won't press you. When you feel ready to confide in me, I will be happy to listen."

From there they returned to the kitchens, where Jenna showed her the small storage room which they had made into their current pantry. Someone had scrubbed it clean before coating the stone walls with a whitish paint, a prudent measure that would help reveal any vermin that might find their way into the stores. Aside from smoked fish and a few freshly-caught game birds they had stored very little meat. Ample bundles of herbs, greenery and root vegetables had been hung from boughs wedged between the stone walls. Some hastily-made wooden boxes held generous heaps of various berries as well. After inspecting everything and seeing no sign of insects or vermin Rosealise nodded her approval.

"You'll want to salt as much of the fish that you wish to keep for winter," she told Jenna as they emerged. "That should better preserve them. Some of the herbs shall fare better after sun-drying. The berries as well, although we might wish to make some into jam or syrups before they over-ripen. I'd love to collect some strawberry leaves for a tisane." She would consult with Mael first, of course, but the work could be started immediately. "Why do you look worried now?"

Jenna sighed. "Honestly, I don't know how to do any of those things."

"Oh," Rosealise said, a bit surprised. "Well it seems that I do." She was also dismayed at how quickly such knowledge had come to her when she remembered nothing of the life in which she had learned it. "I should be quite the glock when it comes to rebuilding a castle, however, so I shall leave that work in your capable hands." She gazed around them and sighed. "You've no makings for a pot of tea. But with the herbs and berries I might manage a decent tisane." She paused and turned back to Jenna. "If I may?"

"Please do," the other woman said. "And teach me while you're at it?"

Chapter Six

AS SHE HAD predicted to herself, it took another few days for Rosealise to become accustomed to her new living arrangements. The rather haphazard manner in which the Mag Raith ran their household vexed her most. Everything necessary for daily life had to be improvised or done without until a substitute could be hand-fashioned. They lived completely isolated at the castle, with no neighbors. While nature provided an abundance of raw materials, they had few tools and little experience with tackling domestic tasks, as she discovered one morning when she and Jenna came into the hall.

There they found Mael, his head and shoulders black with soot as he worked a large branch into the flue above the central hearth.

"Gracious, sir, that won't do," Rosealise said, hurrying over to the seneschal to stop his inexpert cleaning.

As soon as he drew the branch out of the hearth, she took it from him. The scent of him quickly enveloped her, as warm and cozy as if the fire still burned. Her hands itched to touch him in a most unseemly manner, to feel his firm, smooth skin gliding under her palms. Surely, she'd never been like this in the past that she couldn't recall. It was most disconcerting.

Mael smiled at her in such a way that made her toes curl inside her boots. "Fair morning, my lady."

The sound of his voice hummed inside Rosealise's breast with butterfly wings. They stared at each other until Jenna cleared her throat, as if to remind them of her presence.

"Forgive my wool-gathering. You must bundle with cording a great heap of holly to pass *down* through the chimney from its stack."

Rosealise brushed at the soot on his sleeves and glanced up at the thatching. "If one may safely ascend to such heights, that is."

"Aye, my lady." Before she could say another word Mael hurried out.

"Well, it seems I know how to sweep a chimney as well as insult a man's hard work." Rosealise gave Jenna a rueful look. "I should better explain the method to him. Would you please excuse me?"

Jenna smiled. "Of course."

Walking quickly in the chieftain's roomy pantaloons required a discreet adjustment of the cord belt Jenna had improvised for her. Rosealise had not yet seen any spare cloth she might sew into a proper skirt, and suspected her hosts had a sore need for fabric and dunnage. Although she had no memory of making any particular clothes, the methods seemed abundantly clear to her.

As she passed through the kitchens, the scanty amount of cook pots and utensils concerned her anew. It seemed the Mag Raith and Jenna had come to Dun Chaill with little more than their horses. While feeding and caring for five men and two women could not compare to running a large house filled with staff, certain necessities needed to be addressed.

Someone truly needs to help Mael by taking charge of the household.

Since Rosealise was more confident now in her abilities, it might as well be her. She liked to work, which made her wonder if she had been in service. The prospect of taking some of the burden from the seneschal's shoulders also felt entirely right. Moreover, the thought of teaching Jenna such skills pleased her immensely. Having the temerity to instruct the younger woman should have seemed presumptuous, and yet the notion felt very natural, as if she had often performed such tutoring in her vanished past.

Perhaps I taught other household staff. I might have been a cook or a housekeeper.

Outside the roofless passage leading to the garden Rosealise found Mael carrying a huge armful of thorny-leafed branches. Her heart girlishly skipped as she met his darkly bejeweled gaze. Could she never be near him without feeling such palpitations?

"Here you are, Seneschal." She forced herself to look at what he'd collected. "Gracious, that is certainly a generous bundle of holly."

A coil of rope Mael had tucked under his arm fell to the ground as he peered over the heap. "'Tis plenty in the pinewoods. I'll fetch more, if needed."

"I'm sure you've gathered enough to sweep every chimney in the place," Rosealise assured him. "Would you place that on the ground, that I may show you the portion to be bound, and the method?"

He lowered the holly to the grass, but when he straightened several branches clung to his tunic, scattering the rest. He tried to pry a branch away, only to tear the fabric and prick his fingers.

"You are too impatient. Do allow me." Rosealise went to him and began carefully removing the detritus. The excuse to put her hands on Mael pleased her as much as being so close to him, for she could discreetly breathe in his warm, fetching scent. "You're a very obliging gentleman."

He seemed now fascinated by her efforts. "'Tis plain you ken more of such work."

"Unhappily I cannot attest to that with any real certainty." Once she had freed the last branch and dropped it on the pile, she saw a bloody scratch on his neck. "Oh, you're hurt."

"'Tis naught."

He bent down to retrieve the rope, and his arm brushed against the side of her leg.

The sunlight vanished, leaving Rosealise blind and alone. When she blinked, the blackness remained, and all manner of odd thoughts filled her head. She marveled that it no longer hurt, for one thing, and yet she had been in no pain before this moment. She had the sense of having been thrown and injured quite recently, which seemed odd given that she had been standing beside...beside...

Why couldn't she remember the dear fellow's name?

The darkness about her seemed deeper than that of sleep. For a terrifying moment she wondered if all she had known before had been but a dream, or the fancies brought on by death. Had she been buried alive and awakened in her grave?

No, it could not be so. No coffin surrounded her, and she could breathe.

The use of her lungs brought another disagreeable discovery: stench. The brackish, rotting smell that came with every breath made her stomach heave. She gathered that the odor came from the wet, soft muck squishing under her hands. Perhaps she had rolled into a bog. If that were the case, then why couldn't she remember it? Where was the sky? Even at the darkest hours there should be stars.

Managing to push herself up, Rosealise gasped as cold pressed in on her. This place might smell of the swamp, but it was as cold as a January blizzard. She went still as she heard chains rattling and made out the shape of another looming over her.

"Show yerself," a man said, growling the words in a threadbare voice.

"I wish I could, but I fear I cannot find a candle to do so." Drawing on all the courage she could muster, Rosealise reached out. Her fingers touched warm flesh, which seemed to be a large, muscular leg clad in badly-ripped pantaloons. The side of her hand grazed shackles around his ankle, making her wonder if she'd been put in some sort of prison. "Would you help me up, please, sir?"

"Aye, lass."

He grunted as he reached down, and from the strain of his muscles and the sounds of the chains, she perceived he had been somehow restrained. Carefully he lifted her, holding her even after she found her footing. Being unable to see his face frightened her as much as their surroundings, but from the care he took with her she guessed him to be a gentle soul.

"I don't understand this," she murmured. "I suffered a dreadful accident, I think, and was badly hurt. Then I woke up here, which I cannot imagine the aftermath of such a thing. Where am I?"

He said nothing for so long Rosealise wondered if he knew. Had they both been imprisoned here? Why had he been shackled? Was he dangerous? She couldn't make sense of their predicament. At the very least men and women were never incarcerated together.

"'Tis the underworld," he said at last, his rough voice shredding the last word. "And we made slaves of the demons here."

Not a prison, she decided, but perhaps Bedlam. "Why should they enslave us?"

"I cannae tell ye that." He sighed. "Mayhap 'twill never be revealed to us."

His Scottish accent sounded very thick, and he used the countrified speech of a farmer or laborer. Thankfully Rosealise understood him and kept her voice soft so as not to further agitate the poor soul.

"You must know something about these demons."

"Naught ye'll wish to ken. Brace yerself now, lass." His hand stroked up and down her back as if he were petting her. "Demons stole ye from your time. Ye must have seen them. They've the visages of gods and fly through the sky with wings. But they are as evil as nothing ye may imagine. They steal the souls of the helpless and the dying and bring them to this place. Here they torment us and use us for their own amusement."

He spoke of things beyond her understanding, and yet she trusted every word he uttered. She might not remember what had happened to her, but she knew he was correct.

"How long have you been down here?" she asked.

"I cannae tell ye." He wrapped his arms around her, hoping to give her some warmth. Her shivering had died away, and the desperate clutch of her hands was no longer as tight. "Ye must be brave now."

That had always been expected of her, and she resented it now. Alone, with a mostly-naked man in a pit of despair, she should be permitted to dissolve into hysterics. Yet his embrace staved off the panic that wanted to erupt from her. Indeed, she had never felt this safe or protected. Recklessly she pressed her cheek against his chest, and listened to the steady, heavy thud of his heart.

Rosealise.

❧

"ROSEALISE."

When Mael saw her eyelashes flutter, the iron fist in his chest finally loosened enough to let him breathe deep. She lay still and unmoving in his arms, but pink slowly warmed her pallid cheeks, and her own breathing steadied.

"I've made a knacker of myself again, haven't I?" she murmured, opening one eye to peer up at him. "How you must despise me."

"Never," Mael told her, and brushed some curly locks back from her brow. She felt warmer to him now, and when she opened her eyes fully, they looked clear. "The fault, 'tis mine. I reckon I unbalanced you."

Rosealise's lips curved. "You certainly accomplished that, Seneschal."

Gods, but how sorely she tempts me.

Mael bent his head a little lower, completely absorbed by the curving perfection of her smile. Her scent washed over him, all snowy light and wind-washed. He imagined kissing her until neither of them could draw a slow breath.

"You've upended me the same, lass."

"I certainly have no intention in that regard. Every time I'm near you, I think…" Her voice trailed off as her gaze shifted past him. "Please don't be alarmed," she said, the softness of her tone becoming brisk again. "I merely swooned and fell. I'm making a terrible habit of it."

Mael turned his head to see Broden standing but an arm's length away. The trapper held a string of brown trout in one hand and two hares dangling from the other. The rapt manner in which he was staring at Rosealise made a surge of anger flare in Mael.

"Fetch some water for the lady, Brother," Mael told him.

For a moment Broden looked as if he might argue. Indeed, from the tension in his shoulders and the narrowing of his eyes, he appeared ready to fling his catch at Mael's head. He dropped the game and came over to crouch beside Rosealise.

"Shall I carry you inside, my lady?" he demanded, glaring over her head.

"Oh, no, sir. I shall recover in a moment." She patted his hand. "If you'd be kind and bring some water for me, I'd be so grateful."

Without another word the trapper rose, turned on his heel and retreated into the kitchens.

"That gentleman seems quite out of sorts," Rosealise said, gripping Mael's arm to pull herself upright. "Have I said something or done something to cause his suspicion of you?"

"No, and dinnae worry on it. 'Tis but Broden's surly nature." As she tucked her legs under her to stand, he held her a little more tightly. "Slowly now, lass."

With his help she stood, and then leaned against him for another moment. By then the trapper had returned with a cup of water, which she accepted with another murmur of thanks.

"What made you fall, my lady?" Broden asked, again looking at Mael as if he suspected him to be the cause.

"A flash of reminiscence, I believe. I was in a terrible, dark place. A pit, I think." After taking a sip from the cup she added, "Someone else had been chained there, a Scotsman, like you chaps, and he told me we'd been enslaved. I could not see his face. He seemed in terrible straits, but he behaved very kindly to me." She glanced from Broden to Mael and back again. "Could it have been one of you?"

The trapper hesitated before he looked

away and shrugged. "I've no' recalled being in a pit with you."

"'Tis the same for me," Mael admitted. Since Rosealise had arrived, Mael had spent much of his time trying to drag anything about her from the dark abyss of his memory. All that did was make him doubt they'd ever met. "Come now." He put a supporting arm around her. "You should rest inside."

"Yes, that seems sensible." She reached out to Broden as they passed him, and touched his sleeve. "Perhaps you could tie together a bundle of that holly there, sir. It should be tidy and small enough to pass through a chimney. If you would, leave a generous length of rope on each side for pulling."

Mael expected the trapper to refuse. Broden disliked being given orders, especially by females, and he despised such work. But the other man simply nodded and knelt by the holly.

Inside the kitchens Rosealise sat on the stool by the hearth and sighed with relief. "I still feel somewhat weak in the knees." She caught and squeezed his hand. "I fear I've forced you to play my savior again. What must you think of me?"

"You're as lovely as moonlight on a still loch." He crouched down before her, unable to stop himself from confessing his true feelings. "I cannae fathom why I think on you so much. 'Tis foolishness, for I ken I've naught to offer you. All females look upon me and see but a brute."

"You, a brute? Codswallop." She touched his cheek. "You don't frighten me in the slightest degree, my dear sir."

Her hand on his face sent a surge of heated, weighty desire through him. "Call me by my name. To hear thus on your lips enchants me."

Before she could reply Edane came into the kitchens, stopping at the sight of them.

"I dinnae mean to intrude," the archer said to Mael, "but Domnall needs your aid felling that alder in the granary." He glanced at Rosealise. "You're well, my lady?"

"Quite so, although I have the headache again, and I think the beginnings of a cough," she admitted, touching her temple. "I hope I've not caught a chill. Jenna mentioned to me that you've had training as a healer. Perhaps you know of some treatment?"

Mael winced, for Edane hated any reminder that he had been intended to become a shaman. "I'll make you a brew for it, lass," he said, rising to go to the hearth.

"No' too hot," the archer told him, and came to draw Rosealise to her feet.

She sighed. "I do wish you could reveal what's the matter with me."

His expression changed. "I suspect 'tis no' a bodily pain you suffer. If you'd close your eyes, my lady?"

As soon as she did Edane lifted his hands, holding them on either side of her face without touching her. Mael blinked as he heard the archer murmuring under his breath. The shimmer of magic engulfed his hands as well as Rosealise's hair. Never once in all the centuries they had served together had Mael seen Edane use his shaman talent before a stranger.

"'Tis an enchantment," the archer muttered as he turned his fingers to sift them through the shimmer. "Old, mayhap ancient. No' worked by Pritani or druid magic." He frowned. "'Tis fashing me. I vow I've felt the same spelltrace before now."

"When?" Mael demanded. "Where?"

"I cannae tell you, but I've no' the skill nor power to break it." Slowly he drew his hands back. "Open your eyes now, my lady."

Rosealise did so and touched her temple. "My head feels a little better. You claim this was done with magic?"

"Aye. You've been bespelled, likely to forget all you ken of the past," Edane said frankly. "The same I'll wager 'twas done to Jenna before she left the underworld. She came to us aware of naught more but her name."

"Who would wish to do such a thing to me?" Rosealise asked.

"'Tis the work of the demons, I reckon. Dinnae strive to remember, for 'twill cause more pain as the spell works to prevent such. Mayhap in time your past shall come back to you, as Jenna's did to her." The archer blinked a few times, and then frowned as he regarded Mael. "Shall I tell the chieftain you'll aid him?"

"Aye, but give me another moment with

the lady, Brother." He watched the archer leave before he turned to see Rosealise staring into the flames. Her mouth had gone tight, as if she worried now. "I should find Jenna and ask her to sit with you a while."

"No, I will be myself again." She rubbed her brow. "If only I knew why I was made to forget. What might I have known that would imperil the like of demons?"

At that moment Broden entered the kitchens with a neatly-tied bunch of holly.

"'Tis done, my lady," he said, setting the bundle down by the hearth. He stared at it for a moment, his brow furrowing as if he wasn't sure of what it was.

"How clever of you to finish so quickly." Rosealise went over to inspect his work, and patted his shoulder. "Jolly good knots there. We will need them to hold the branches together during the sweeping. This rope, is it sturdy enough to pull?"

"Oh, aye, 'twillnae break," the trapper said, his scowl vanishing. "I wound it myself for bridles and such."

"Smashing," she said. "Here is what we will do with it to clean the stacks."

As the lady explained the method to him, making graceful gestures with her hands, Mael was astounded again. Broden not only listened to every word she said, but he seemed entirely set on performing the task. The same Broden who, Mael recalled, had such a hatred of soot that he rarely used his own hearth when they had lived among the Moss Dapple.

"My lady," Mael said, interrupting their discussion. "Might I–"

"You needn't bother with this. Broden and I will attend to the chimneys," Rosealise said, touching his hand. "Please, do go and assist your chieftain now."

Mael didn't want to leave her alone with the trapper, and yet he turned and walked out of the kitchens. As he strode toward the granary, he tried to stop and turn around, but his feet kept moving. Then something he'd said to her came back to him, but with far less pleasure than when he'd uttered it.

To hear thus on your lips enchants me.

At the entrance to the granary he ducked inside and found the chieftain sharpening a two-handled axe.

"You look as if you've been chewing thistles," Domnall said, testing the edge of the blade with one thumb. "Have you some grief to relate?"

"None," Mael replied, but he had suspicions. He also sensed that the lady had no idea of what she could do. "After we fell the tree, might I speak with your wife?"

Chapter Seven

✦

FROM HIS BLIND in the ridges Cul watched a herd of female red deer encircle their white-spotted fawns as they fed in a patch of succulent wild herbs. Thistledown floated around them, adding a dreamy softness to the air. So close he could count their tiny white patches, he inspected the fattened flesh under their summer-bright hides. The largest of the hinds ignored the feed to keep watch for predators while the fawns grazed, but the precautions Cul had taken made him invisible to them. The prospect of fresh meat had tempted him to emerge from hiding, but dragging even a small carcass through the tunnels would take too long. Leaving the remains behind risked exposing his presence to the enemy.

They must never know until the last possible moment that all they suffered had been Cul's doing.

His gaze shifted to the faint smear of darkness on the western horizon. Within that coming storm would fly the Sluath, as well-fed as the deer. He knew from the mingled scents and blood trace he had found in the glen that they had done something to the druid that now served them. They had not killed the mortal, however, which intrigued him. The demons loathed his kind, and had no reason or will to deny themselves even the most dismal of amusements.

If the druid had chosen to share in them, Cul would show no such restraint.

He retreated into the cave, feeling the remnants of power left behind raking his flesh like so many tiny, invisible claws. To his great pleasure the Sluath had grown careless over time, likely due to their rightful assumption that they had the power to annihilate anything that stood in their way. When he reached the shimmering gate to the underworld, his twisted lips parted. It would be nothing for him to step through the barrier and make his way into the depths. Iolar and his demons would have left everything awaiting their pleasure. He could destroy all that they assumed they'd always possess. He could leave them as he had been: alone, outcast, with nothing and no one.

Yet even that couldn't be enough to satisfy him. They had to know his suffering as he had, year by year, decade by decade, century by dreary century.

Once Cul finished his work he made his way over land to his own territory. After the massacre at the village, no mortals but the Mag Raith and their female occupied his lands, so he could chance moving openly in the light. Yet since the hunters had chosen to reside in his castle, he'd been obliged to enter the lower passages from the maze, where the hedges concealed him. Damage to the trap there made him pause and inspect his construct.

Sluath enchantment lingered in the air, but so did the smallest trace of mortal blood.

Following the latter drew him to a brown-stained patch of bramble. From the scant amount of blood she'd left behind, it seemed that the female hadn't been badly wounded by the maze's lethal magic. No doubt one of the hunters had rescued her. They had proven as protective as the watchful deer. He caught a flake of the blood and tasted it, his distorted mouth forming a sneering smile.

Luscious, but also plagued. He would have to move quickly to use this one.

Cul parted the hedges and soil covering his stone door, and opened it to descend into his lair. He took the passage leading to his archive, where he had recorded the progress he had made with his work. Scraped hides covered the stone floor, each burned with lines representing tunnels and gates no mortal had ever beheld. He knelt down to scratch out the arching mark representing the cave where he had just labored, and then straightened to survey the rest of the hides. Every other arch etched into the map had been similarly obliterated. He'd been sure of it, but to see the proof with his own eyes sent a wave of savage delight through him.

Those who had preyed on him would now become the prey.

Cul capered around the room, his ungainly body colliding with the hard walls as he allowed his glee full reign. Parchment scrolls fell from their shelves to bounce along with his limping steps, and crackled as he crushed them under his feet. Dust rose in small, dull clouds from the oldest as they disintegrated. None of them mattered anymore now that he had completed the work. The demons would soon know the desperation of the outcast, the reviled, the hunted. They would search in vain for an escape, which in time would lead them to Dun Chaill, and then to him. A thought occurred to him that stopped him in his tracks.

He had not yet tested the lure for his final trap.

Limping out of the archive, Cul shook off the dust before he made his way up to his observation posts. There, his chest heaving, he put his clear eye to one of the spy holes and looked into the reflecting glass. He could use them only during the day, for the other glasses required sunlight to send down images from the keepe far above him.

Where are they?

He spied the new female in the great hall, where she stood tugging on a rope hanging from inside one of the hearths. Soot and detritus rained down on her hands and arms, but she continued the work until the showering filth ceased. She coughed several times before she placed her head in the hearth and called up the chimney. Cul couldn't hear her, but he read her words from the movements of her lips.

That's very good, Broden. I believe we've finished.

"No, woman," Cul murmured, thinking of the traps he might employ. "You've much more work to do before you depart the mortal realm."

From there he returned to his archive, and took a blank sheet of parchment and ink from the stores of what he had made himself since coming to Dun Chaill. He would have to be clever now, but careful. More than once he had underestimated the canniness of mortals, and to do so now might spring his trap too early.

He stoked the hearth in his chamber before he took to the desk he had built even before the archive existed. The chair he'd fashioned to fit his distorted body creaked as he lowered himself onto it. He spread out the parchment and weighed it down. Carefully he uncorked the bottle of ink and poured a small measure over the center of the blank scroll. It puddled in the air just above the scraped skin.

"Now," he murmured, watching a shimmer engulf the murky blue liquid. "Show them all they have not found."

A quill made of dark green light appeared above the ink, dipped itself into the puddle, and began to draw.

Chapter Eight

❧❀❧

THAT AFTERNOON MAEL asked Jenna to walk with him down to the stream. As they made their way through the forest, she spoke of her plans to alter the waterfall room to make it safe for their use.

"It's the last deathtrap in the keepe, but it'll be easy enough to deactivate. Once Domnall and I remove the levers from the sluice doors, and the shut-off valves from the ducts, it should make a pretty good bath house." A soft smile played over her lips. "The water is the perfect temperature."

He tried not to think of Rosealise bathing in a cascade, yet his mind would dwell on nothing else. Everything about the Englishwoman fascinated him. He'd even considered saying nothing about what he discovered that morning. He wished to protect the lady, just as he had Jenna when he had first glimpsed her using her magic. But the architect had been fully aware of what she had been about, and he had to think of the others now.

When they reached the banks, Jenna sat down on a flat rock. She looked out over the sparkling currents before she met his gaze.

"We didn't come here to talk about my renovation plans. What's on your mind?"

Mael told her, beginning with his reactions to Rosealise's requests and adding what he'd observed Edane and Broden do for her. It felt like a betrayal, but he knew that to conceal it might lead to something far worse. When he finished Jenna glanced back at Dun Chaill, her brows drawing together.

"You really think Rosealise is capable of something like that? I think we would have noticed."

"I dinnae reckon 'tis noticed or felt. Hasnae she done the same to you, and you couldnae resist?"

"No, but…" She paused and frowned. "It

is odd, how much I've told her about us. Any time I'm with her and she asks me something, I answer her. Even when it's something she's not yet prepared to hear. But it wasn't deliberate on her part. She's very easy to talk to, and it's nice to have another woman around the castle."

"You didnae ken you could take on ghost form," Mael pointed out. "I dinnae blame the lady for it. I vow she's no' at all aware of it."

"Okay, for the sake of argument, let's say you're right." Jenna cocked her head. "Why are you telling me instead of Domnall?"

"I must advise the chieftain," he admitted. "Yet I would first be sure. We must see her use her power where all may behold it. I ken you'd keep the scheme to yourself until 'tis done, and after you could aid Rosealise in how to reckon with such a gift."

"You're a nice man, Mael," she said and nodded. "All right, I'm in. How do we do this?"

"I must be the one to test her." Mael thought of the few things he abhorred. "Vetch. I cannae abide the taste of it. Nor can I stomach it. Even when I didnae ken 'twas in the pottage the *dru-wids* prepared, 'twould make me boak."

"Well, we've got plenty in the garden." Jenna rubbed her knuckles against her chin. "I think I know how to manage it." She told him of her notion, and then reached out and touched his arm. "You're sure you want to put yourself through this?"

"'Tis better we ken," he assured her.

Back at the stronghold they skirted the great hall and entered the kitchens through the side passage. While Jenna prepared the cook pot, Mael went out to the garden to collect the vetch. Brambles had grown over the gap in the hedge where he had jumped out with Rosealise, but when he stepped nearer the branches parted to form another opening.

"'Tis another bespelled trap," Edane said as he waded through the overgrown herbs to join him. "'Twill do the same at every side wherever we draw near. I've told the others."

Mael glanced at the archer, who held a spade fashioned from a branch and a piece of slate.

"What do you now?"

"I saw a mound of stone and dirt in the

forest," Edane said, nodding toward the south. "'Tis too shaped to be natural, and too high for a grave site. I feel no magic from it. Why do you gather that? You ken how swift vetch sours your belly."

Mael tugged out some stalks. "'Tis what Jenna calls an 'experiment.'" He eyed the archer. "'Twould oblige me to have your aid with it."

Edane frowned. "What manner of mischief do you?"

"Naught 'twill harm anyone," he assured him. He didn't want to condemn Rosealise yet without proof, so he added, "'Tis more of a trial, to ken what we reckon to be truth. I'll tell you the rest once I speak to Jenna."

The archer accompanied him back to the kitchens, where Mael gave the plants to Jenna. She chopped them and brought a handful to the pottage she had cooking over the fire.

"No, Brother," Mael told Edane when he tried to stop her. "'Tis necessary to prove a notion. Only ken I shallnae willingly touch that pottage."

"Why should you?" The archer frowned.

"By the Gods, Mael, I cannae fathom
your wit."

"'Tis no' a jest." He regarded the chieftain's wife. "I must tell him all, but nowhere
we may be heard. We'll return in time for the
evening meal."

Jenna gave him a sympathetic look. "All
right. Just be ready for anything."

Chapter Nine

ROSEALISE GLANCED AROUND the great hall with some satisfaction. With Broden's help she'd swept three of the chimneys before Jenna came out to join them.

"You've been busy," the chieftain's wife said as she regarded the neat piles of rotting leaves, abandoned birds' nests and twigs they had cleared. "If you don't mind stopping for a bit, it's time to feed these guys."

"Of course." Rosealise eyed her blackened hands. The sight of them made her feel an urge to cough again, but swallowing dispelled it. "Broden and I will have a wash first, and then I'll help you."

The other woman eyed the soot-covered trapper before she nodded.

After a good scrub at the kitchen basin Rosealise went to the hearth to check the bubbling pot of soup Jenna had made, and took in the scrumptious aroma.

"This smells delicious."

"It's mostly quail and wild carrot, with some herbs. An old Pritani recipe that everyone loves." Jenna nodded at a stack of broad wooden bowls and a pile of carved spoons. "If you'll set the table, I'll bring out the pot."

In the great hall Broden and Domnall had assembled the trestle table, on which Rosealise placed the bowls and spoons. The primitive place settings would have looked a little more civilized with some napkins, but perhaps in time they could purchase or trade for such niceties.

I don't wish to leave here. The thought should have startled her, but it seemed entirely natural. She had been made welcome by good, kind souls who seemed the very best of friends, and of course there was Mael. *Perhaps he will ask me to stay.*

As all the other men arrived, Jenna came to her.

"Would you ask Mael to try the soup first? He told me how to make it, so I'd like to know what he thinks."

Rosealise smiled. "Of course, but I'm sure it's very appetizing."

She sat down beside the tracker and took his bowl to ladle in a healthy portion of the pottage. When she sat it in front of him, however, he merely shook his head.

"Jenna desires your good opinion of her cooking," she reproved him gently, and touched his arm. "Do try some of the soup."

Mael's hand shook oddly as he picked up his spoon and dipped it into the bowl. Just as he lifted it to his lips Jenna came over and snatched the spoon away. He then took Rosealise's spoon and used it as if nothing had happened.

"My lady," Edane said, as if in warning.

"Tell him to stop," Jenna said to her.

"Whatever for?" Rosealise protested, astounded by the presumption.

By then Mael had swallowed a mouthful of the soup. His lips thinned, and he rose to his feet. Without a word he fled the hall, and the distant sound of his retching drifted back to them.

Edane muttered under his breath before he got up and went after the tracker.

"Rosealise, please don't say anything else until after I explain," Jenna said quickly. "Mael told me earlier today that the taste of vetch makes him very sick. He never touches it, or any food that contains it. All the other hunters know this, too. That's why I put a bunch of vetch in the soup."

"What say you?" Domnall said and he rose and peered into the cook pot before giving her a narrow look. "You ken you'd poison him?"

"Mael asked me to do it. He even went out to the garden to pick the vetch for me. He also promised me that he wouldn't eat any of the soup." She shifted her gaze to Rosealise. "But you told him to try it, and he did. Just as you told Broden to help you sweep the chimneys, and Edane to use his shaman training. Neither of them would have voluntarily done those things. You persuaded them to do it against their will."

Broden pressed a hand over his eyes, and Kiaran's expression darkened.

"I cannot make out your meaning, my dear," Rosealise said slowly. "Why should you blame me for what these men did?"

"We believe you have the ability to persuade anyone to do what you say while you're touching them," Jenna said. "It may have been given to you during your time in the underworld."

A laugh burst from Rosealise. "That's utterly absurd." She saw the way the men were regarding her now and felt a sudden dread. "Do understand, I'm aware that I'm rather a forthright soul. Whatever I did in my life must have required some instruction of others, for I seem very comfortable with it. But for me to inflict such coercion on others by touch? It simply isn't possible."

"You must show her your power, *luaidh*," the chieftain said gently to his wife.

Jenna bowed her head, and her body began to fade from view. When she looked as if she might dissolve entirely, she stood up and walked through the table. On the other side she grew solid again as she met Rosealise's horrified gaze.

"My ability allows me to move through solid objects." She nodded at Domnall. "My husband can move faster than the eye can see. The other men all have their own extraordinary talents, too."

"I will prove you wrong," Rosealise said, rising from the table and moving to where the trapper sat. "Broden, I'm sure you helped me with the chimney sweeping because you wished to." She patted his shoulder. "You've been ever so kind, all day. Please, assure them of this."

"I wished to help Rosealise," Broden said through his clenched teeth.

Jenna sighed. "You persuaded him again by touching his shoulder and telling him to assure us of what you said."

This was completely ridiculous, but thankfully her innocence would be proven in another moment. She removed her hand.

"Very well. Broden, please speak the truth. Did you wish to help me with the work?"

"No." The trapper's expression turned to disgust as he looked down at the soot staining his tunic. "I'd rather eat raw vetch than do such work."

Rosealise froze. "If it was not your desire to do so, then why did you?"

Broden shrugged. "When you spoke, I thought of naught else but what you wished." He made a harsh sound. "You enslave with your words, my lady."

A miserable shame filled Rosealise as she slowly backed away. "It would seem you are correct in your suspicions, Jenna." Her face was burning hot, and her hands shook as she pressed her cold fingers against her cheeks. "I must beg forgiveness from all of you. Truly I had no idea I'd forced anyone to do my bidding. The notion that I could is absolutely abhorrent to me."

"It's all right," Jenna said quickly. "Now that you're aware of your persuasion power, you can learn to control it. We'll help you."

"When I might control you with a touch?" She shook her head. "You've been so thoughtful and attentive, and I've done this terrible thing. I might have hurt one of you. I must go at once. Somehow I'll find my way to my people."

"They've no' been born yet, my lady," Domnall told her, and glanced at Jenna, who nodded. "When the Sluath hunt mortals to enslave they move through time. They stole my wife from the twenty-first century. Jenna believes you lived in the nineteenth. The Mag Raith came from the first. Here and now, 'tis the fourteenth century."

What he'd said stunned Rosealise, but everything she hadn't understood about the men—their speech, primitive mannerism, and comfort with the lack of amenities—all became suddenly comprehensible.

"Is this what you've been keeping from me?" she asked the chieftain's wife.

"Yes," Jenna said, "but only because we didn't want to upset you anymore than you already were. We would have told you eventually."

Even when deceiving her they had been kind. "Jolly good of you. Do be assured that I won't cause any more trouble."

Rosealise fled the hall, stopping only when she encountered Mael and Edane in the outer passage. Perspiration covered the seneschal's pale face, and he had an arm around the archer's shoulders as if he might collapse without the support. He'd treated her with such gentleness and consideration, and in turn she'd made him suffer.

"You needn't worry about this happening again," she said to Mael. "I'm so dreadfully sorry."

She rushed out of the keepe, and hurried toward the forest. Not knowing where she would go or what she would do didn't matter. She simply needed to escape, and find a quiet place where she wouldn't impose herself on anyone. There she could collapse and weep and rail at the unkindness of her fate.

Just before she reached the trees a blur rushed past her. It stopped and became Domnall, standing directly in her path. When she tried to go around him his body blurred, and he blocked her again.

"Dinnae run from us, my lady," the chieftain said, putting his hand on her arm.

Jenna had spoken the truth about her husband as well, Rosealise thought dully. "Please move out of my way." As he immediately stepped to one side she groaned. "Forgive me, sir. I did not intend– Oh, how could they do this to me? And why would they take me from my own time to bring me here to yours?"

"I cannae tell you," Domnall said. "The Sluath took the Mag Raith without reason, and when we awoke all we cared for had died or vanished. 'Twas when I discovered my quickness, by running three leagues in as many breaths. Had I no' stopped myself, I'd have gone over a cliff. 'Twill seem unbearable now, but you've strength and courage. You'll find the will to live with it."

"Perhaps, but you cannot trust me. Indeed, Chieftain, I have absolutely no more faith in myself." She was so wretched she wanted to weep. "Would you be so kind as to offer my sincere apologies again to Mael? I never dreamt of making him suffer so."

Heavy footsteps approached, and the chieftain looked past her. "Tell him yourself, and stay, Dash. We need you here."

Dash.

The fondness with which he renamed her both comforted and bewildered Rosealise as she watched him go. She could not bring herself to face the man standing behind her, but courtesy demanded she say something.

"You needn't ask me to stay, really," she said as evenly as she could. "You owe me nothing, and I certainly cannot say the same. After what I've done, what I can do, it's quite clear that I must depart."

""'Tis no such thing," Mael said. "Willnae you look at me?"

His hands touched her shoulders, and gently guided her around toward him. His breath smelled of mint rather than sick, and she was relieved to see his color had returned. His warmth engulfed her like a fond embrace. Everything inside her wanted to be here with him, and nowhere else. To know she'd harmed him, however, made her insides curdle.

"How much you must despise me," she said, and ducked her head. "Not that I wish you to." Meeting his gaze again took all her nerve, and when she saw the sorrow there it defeated the last of her thin courage. "Mael, I must leave. Surely you must... Oh, this is wretched, that I might force you to do anything with a touch."

"Listen to me first, my lady. Since boyhood I've been this great hulk, just as my sire was. Fargas lived to make others cower before him." He glanced down at himself. "Yet 'twas never in my nature to act the brute as he would. I didnae care to forever drink and brawl as he did. 'Twas my aim to be caring and friendly. My people still kept their distance and made me feel an outcast. No matter what I did, I ever frightened the young, the small, and the weak."

"How you look isn't your fault," she said, feeling now as if her heart would break.

"Aye, and nor 'tis yours, this persuasion power. We've all some burden to carry, my lady." He took her hand, as if he meant to lead her back to Dun Chaill. "Permit us help you to bear it."

Rosealise knew what she was about to do was yet another cruelty, but she swore to herself it would be her last.

"I wish you to tell me the truth, Seneschal. Do you and the others truly want me to stay?"

Mael smiled. "Aye, my lady."

Relief poured through her already-ragged emotions, overwhelming her. Rosealise fell against him and burst into tears.

Strong arms lifted her and carried her into the cool shadow of an oak. There Mael sat with her on his lap, and held her, making low, soothing sounds as he stroked her arm and back.

Finally, Rosealise's sobs subsided, but she couldn't move an inch.

"Look at me," she said, sighing the words. "I should make a stuffed bird laugh, or fill a tear bottle to the brim."

Mael tipped up her chin. "You keep too much bottled, my lady."

To show her gratitude, Rosealise kissed his cheek. A simple gesture, and yet the moment her lips touched his skin a cacophony of unseemly sensations resonated inside her. By its own volition her hand crept up around his neck to stroke his thick bright hair. More of the touching coaxed her mouth to wander until it touched the corner of his. At the same time her thighs tightened and the most baffling liquid heat pooled between them.

Mael didn't move, but his eyes closed, and he made a low, rough sound.

Rosealise didn't want to speak, not when her touch could be made a weapon against his will. So she did what felt entirely proper, and brushed her lips over his mouth, then drew back an inch. If he felt the same urgency she did, surely he would—

Mael kissed her.

Oh, but this had to be the most intimate, glorious, shocking thing Rosealise had ever done. Never mind that she couldn't recall her past. None of that mattered in the slightest to her anymore. He caught her sigh of delight with his next inhalation and then put his tongue into her mouth. The sheer carnal hunger he kindled made her moan and shift closer, until Mael fell back and she lay atop him.

Her borrowed pantaloons allowed her to straddle him, and her hair fell around them as she cupped his face with her hands. The devastating kiss raged on. Such passion suffused her now that Rosealise doubted she could stop herself. What more could she ever do that would be as pleasurable as this? Feeling his body under hers, and the stroke of his tongue inside her mouth, and the weight of his hands encircling her waist should be all she ever did again.

When he took hold of her buttocks and shifted her, Rosealise thought she might faint. Just a few layers of fabric separated her throbbing, wet sex from the hard, stiff length of his manhood. He must feel the heat of her on himself, surely, and know how wicked she was. All she could think was how it would feel to take all that hard flesh inside herself, and glory to it stroking her from within, and more kisses and touching, both of them naked and feverish with it.

How could you know of this?

The shock of the thought made Rosealise end the dizzying kiss to raise up and look into Mael's eyes. The bronze there had gone so dark it looked like onyx, and every muscle on his big body was knotted beneath the yielding softness of her own. Yet as inviting and arousing as it was to look upon him, she knew she had never kissed this man before now.

Mael looked all over her face. "Lass?"

How could she tell him when she couldn't remember the man who had been her lover? It might have been him, or anyone.

"We must not do this now, my dear sir."

With some effort she climbed off him and

walked a short distance away to compose herself. However Mael didn't wait for her to do so, and joined her.

"If 'twas unwanted, you'd but to say, lass." Immediately he grimaced. "Forgive me, I ken you wouldnae use your power now—"

"It's not that." Odd that he called her "my lady" when being polite, and "lass" when he spoke from his heart. She much preferred the latter. "If you would give me a moment to collect myself, please. It's evident that I must speak carefully."

He waited beside her and together they watched the stream rush by. Rosealise hated feeling the fade of the desires aching inside her. But once her body cooled her mind cleared, and she could regard the tracker without too much temptation tugging at her.

"Thank you, Seneschal. Please understand that I wished to kiss you," she told him. "I'm also convinced that we've never kissed before today. Yet the other matters that would naturally follow such a kiss... I confess, these are known to me. I cannot name my lover, or even recall his face, but from what I imagine... I know that I gave myself to him fully."

"I wish I might say 'twas me," he told her.

"As do I." She glanced at him. "Until I'm certain that I'm free to do so, I cannot offer you more than my friendship. I regret this deeply."

"Dinnae. 'Tis plain you've an honorable heart." Mael held out his hand. "Walk back with me."

The sting of tears made her blink quickly. He understood, and still did not fear her touch. It made her feel safe and cherished as nothing else would.

As they made their way back to the castle, Rosealise found herself brooding on the brief memory of the chained man in the darkness of the pit. She wanted to believe it had been Mael who had helped her, but the prisoner's voice had been different—harsher, almost grating.

Just as Broden's is.

Chapter Ten

EDANE ENTERED THE great hall the next morning to find Jenna and Rosealise seated at the trestle table and engaged in an odd conversation.

"What do you wish me to do?" the chieftain's wife asked as she sat with a platter of oatcakes and two mugs between them. She also held one of the Englishwoman's hands in hers.

"Please do pass the brew," Rosealise said, and then grimaced as Jenna reached for one of the mugs. "No, please ignore that. If you would care to, my dear, do please pass the brew." She coughed a little and cleared her throat. "I beg your pardon. I think yesterday I breathed in more soot than was good for me."

"No problem, and you're doing great," the other woman said, and then caught Edane's gaze. "Fair morning, Archer. We're practicing having contact and conversation without Rosealise using her persuasion mojo. Would you like some breakfast?"

"Please, do join us," Rosealise said, touching his arm, and then added quickly, "if you would wish to, sir."

Edane held up the spade he'd fashioned. "My wish in truth, my lady, 'tis to go digging in the forest." He helped himself to some oatcakes. "But I'll aid you with the practice when I return."

"Thank you, sir." The Englishwoman cleared her throat and regarded Jenna. "Blazes, but I cannot abide this tickle in my throat. Might I beg a spoonful of that honey Kiaran found, if it can be spared?"

The trek to the mound he'd discovered took some time, but Edane enjoyed the walk. The spring had brought out a bounty of greenery and flowers in the forest, making it into an endless bower of beauty. Being indoors reminded him of his boyhood, and too many days and nights spent training in the shaman's *broch* or by his ritual fire. He felt free only out in the fresh air, where he could be in the world as he wished. His desire to hunt had gone, but pursuing the mystery in the forest was proving just as gratifying.

It gave him a new sense of purpose, too. Since coming to Dun Chaill all of the other men had found work suited to their talents and natures. Domnall, Mael, and Jenna had taken charge of turning the ruins into a home for them, and Broden and Kiaran daily provided meat and fish for their meals. Edane had done little more than gather veg and firewood, and that made him feel as he had among their tribe: useless.

At last he reached the trail of his own footsteps leading into the cluster of silver birches that surrounded the high dome of rock and earth. Moss covered it over, but weather had exposed some of the rugged stacked stones chinked with black soil. Although fashioned to appear natural, he'd found the seams between the rocks to be chiseled, indicating the mound had been deliberately built over something.

Some of the old Pritani tribes had buried their dead in mounds made of stone, but marked such places so that others would not disturb the remains. This appeared more like an undercroft for storage, built to withstand time and weather. But if it had been made to provide storage, what had been secreted inside? Food would have surely rotted by now.

'Twill be a trash heap or a privy pit, and I shall seem the fool for digging it out.

Broden would make much of that, and again prod Edane's temper. They'd almost come to blows over the pearls.

Over the centuries Edane had become fascinated with the tiny gems of the sea. One by one, as chance led a trader to cross his path, he'd begun to collect them, especially those rare finds that were perfectly round. Other gems, such as the ones found by Jenna, held no interest for him. Nor did he crave the wealth that they stored. But there was something calming about the subtle beauty of pearls, a lustre born of the moon itself. Ofttimes before taking to his bed, Edane would pour them from their soft leather pouch simply to gaze upon them—until Broden had seen him.

"What do you with your womanly

baubles?" he'd taunted. "String them in your pretty hair?"

Edane quickly gathered them back into their bag and jumped to his feet. "Dinnae you ken the meaning of a closed door?" Heat flushed into his face, as he put the bag behind his back.

"I ken how fetching you must look in them," Broden said, grinning. He stepped forward and held out his hand. "Let us have a look."

As Edane stared at the outstretched hand, cold rage flooded into his chest and his jaw set so hard he thought his teeth would break. Every sinew in his body stretched taut, and he leaned forward on his toes.

"If you ever," he said through barely moving lips, "touch them, I shall gut you." For a moment Broden did nothing, but then he blinked and his smirk slipped. "From your puny bawbag to your hairy chin, my blade 'twill open you like a fattened hog." Broden's eyes narrowed but he lowered his hand. "Now get out," Edane yelled.

In two strides he was across the room and shoving the trapper so hard that the bigger man had to stumble back. Edane slammed the door and bolted it.

Even now, as he thought back on it, blood rose to his cheeks. He needed to stay away from the trapper until the animosity between them returned to a lower simmer.

For now, he would know what lay within the mound before telling anyone of its particulars, so he went to work with the spade at the base of it. Gradually he moved around it as he uncovered the foundation, looking for signs of the entry to the interior. On the back side he exposed a large space between the stones that had been filled in with only soil and pebbles.

He kicked it with his boot and watched the fill crumble. "Aye, you cannae hide from me."

Digging out the entry took a few minutes, and then his spade hit more stone. Dropping down to peer inside the hole he'd made, he saw blocking stones fitted together in an unfamiliar pattern. No stink of rot or waste came from within, so it couldn't be a burial site of late.

"What did you here?" he muttered as he reached in and wedged his fingertips in between two of the flat stones.

With a hard tug he pulled the top stone
out, which proved to be a thin piece of slate.
Setting it to one side, Edane carefully went
about removing the rest. Behind them lay
what appeared to be a sunken room. No dead
stench came from the interior, but as he
peered into the darkness, he made out the
vague outlines of several towering stacks.
Since no one had lived at Dun Chaill for
centuries it couldn't be food stored away for
the cold season.

   'Tis a hoard.

Edane crawled back out of the hole, and
sat back on his haunches as he considered
what next to do. If he went inside and the
mound collapsed, it might become his tomb.
Yet the thought of dying, something he hadn't
pondered in centuries, didn't frighten him now
anymore than it had in his mortal life. Some
things, he knew, were worse.

At last he repeated Broden's favorite
reproof of him. "Dinnae be such a facking
wench."

With dried lichen and a short pine
branch Edane fashioned a torch, then used
his fire steel and dagger to light it. He held it

in front of him as he crawled back into the mound.

Metal gleamed as the torch illuminated the contents of the sunken room. From the opening Edane could see a bewildering variety of objects, from folded tartans to stands of long blades. To one side was a pile of saddles, some with cracked, peeling leather. Swells of bulging satchels and packs sat beside rows of torques, gauntlets and boots. Waxen-topped glazed pottery, and dusty glass bottles sealed with cork, waited to be opened. More unglazed pots, some of them cracked or in pieces, formed piles behind them. Dozens of heavy grain sacks, layered like over-large bricks, covered the back wall of the cache.

Edane eased himself through the opening and dropped down, looking up as some soil sifted down on his head. The top of the mound held firm, however, and as he turned and inspected the hoard, he expected to see bones or a burial cask. For so much wealth to be buried surely the remains of a king had been hidden here, and yet he saw no body.

A dull silver gleam on the ground caught his eye, and he knelt down to pick up a

Roman coin. A dark streak on it flaked off the moment he swept his thumb over its face. The coin had an ancient design, and yet appeared as new as it if had been struck only yesterday.

Edane let it drop and went over to the pile of folded tartans, shaking out the top one and holding it up to the torch's light. A huge dark stain and four long slashes marred the weave. Some of the tartans he examined appeared intact, but others had been stained and rent in similar fashion.

He lifted one torn, stained plaid to his nose, and then he knew.

Edane tossed the tartan over his shoulder and climbed up out of the room. When he emerged from the mound into the sunlight, he backed away from it. He held up the tartan he'd taken and could clearly see the stains on it. The spattering and streaks had been made by blood.

The mound did protect a hoard, one collected from the victims of a savage killer.

❦

MAEL WENT ALONG with Domnall to inspect

Edane's reported discovery, and as the archer showed them the evidence of violence on some of the hoarded goods the chieftain sighed.

"'Twould seem the spoils of an attack. After burying it, the victors likely died elsewhere before they could return to collect it." He shook out one of the tartans, and turned it around. "We'll burn what's marked, but take the rest and stow them in the old pantry. We've dire need of cloth."

"Aye, much may be used," the archer said, "but some looks far older. Those deepest in the hoard have fallen to rot, and 'tis another strangeness." He took out a handful of silver, giving some to both men. "Ken you the stamp?"

"A denarius," Mael said as he held up the bright coin. "'Tis marked with the name of Hadrian Augustus."

Frowning, Domnall examined those he held. "Too new to be from his reign. He died in the first century, when the Romans invaded." He weighed the coins with a shake of his hand. "Seems as heavy as true silver. Forgeries, mayhap."

"'Twas my reckoning, until I found this." Edane's expression turned grim as he bent again to the pile of goods he'd created. He produced a stylized eagle on a perch mounting, fashioned to be affixed to the top of a pole. The polished gold glittered as brightly as the coins. "You ken what 'tis, Chieftain?"

Domnall swore under his breath before he went over to crouch down and peer into the mound.

Mael took the bird, which weighed so much it he nearly dropped it.

"I dinnae ken it, but 'tis solid gold." He'd never seen so much used to make what seemed to him a useless object. "*Dru-wid* made, mayhap?"

"No," the archer said. "'Tis an *aquila*, the standard of the Romans. They marched behind it into battle. 'Twas said they'd die to a man before they let anyone take that from their bearer."

Domnall lit a torch and went into the mound, emerging a short time later.

"'Tis packed to the walls with armor and weapons." He nodded at the eagle. "All appear of Roman design, enough to outfit a hundred soldiers or better."

"They've no' marched through these lands since the time of our tribes," Edane muttered. "'Tis been more than a thousand years since they retreated."

Mael recalled what the villagers in Wachvale had told them of the *kithan*, the monster they believed inhabited Dun Chaill. The local mortals believed the "naught-man" killed anyone who came near the castle. Mael had never been one to be ruled by such superstitious tales, but now he wondered if it had some root in truth. An army of Romans surely could not be defeated by one ordinary mortal, but a powerful druid gone mad might have prevailed with killing magic.

"I'll no' have goods belonging to Romans in the keepe," Domnall said. "Collect what else is fit to be used. I'll send Kiaran to aid you. Mael, with me."

He knew the chieftain wished to say more, but not in front of the archer. Once they had put some distance between them and the mound, Mael said, "I've no liking for how 'twas taken, but 'tis much there that may serve to make life here easier."

"Aye, very useful to us, and kept safe for a thousand years or better. Most opportune." Domnall stopped and glanced back in the direction of the mound. "It stinks of more treachery."

"Edane sensed no magic, and found no traps," Mael reminded him, although now that he thought on it the chieftain's notion made sense. "Mayhap 'tis a cache created and kept for some dire aim, but as the rest of Dun Chaill, forgotten and left to rot. A druid on the dark path, like Galan, could do such."

"Pritani died here." The chieftain rubbed the edge of his jaw before he regarded him. "I saw much in the mound that might have been taken from our tribe, or us. Bone tools, querns, hammer stones and the like. Mayhap Edane has unearthed the old saddles we used when we first came here. My spear tips. That giant square head axe you had forged for hunting grice."

I wasnae hunting pigs.

The sharp teeth of his guilt gnawed at him

for a moment, before a thought occurred to him.

"Mayhap 'twas another tribe that attacked the Romans after the Sluath captured us," the tracker ventured. "They'd take what they could carry and bury the rest." That pondering led to another. "Or the Sluath themselves cached the goods. All I may tell you, 'tis no monster hiding in the castle now, Brother."

Domnall didn't look entirely convinced. "It doesnae stink to me of demon work. Nor the traps we've found in the castle. Yet this place ever wishes to kill us."

"Not by any will. 'Twas left like one of Broden's snares, I reckon, to prey on the unwary." Mael held up his hands and dropped them. "Jenna claims we resolved in the underworld to come to Dun Chaill. With no memory of that vow we yet came. Rosealise fell into the maze, not the ash grove. Mayhap the Gods carved out our path, or 'tis purely by chance, but all led us here."

"Aye." The lines of worry on the chieftain's brow deepened for a moment, and then disappeared. "What say we to our ladies of the mound?"

"All we ken, but only after we burn the stained cloth," Mael told him wryly.

Back at Dun Chaill they found the women working together in the kitchen garden, where they had removed a mound of weeds from the overgrown herbs. Mael smiled when he saw the vetch stalks that had also been discarded.

"How delightful to see you, Chieftain, Seneschal." Rosealise brushed the soil from her hands before she picked up a small sack. "Or fair morning, as you have it. I'm happy to say we'll have enough seed to replant most of the herbs once we've prepared the soil."

"We uncovered another patch of berries, too," Jenna said from somewhere behind. "A huge one where the birds couldn't get at it." She emerged from behind a shrub, holding the edge of her tunic out to keep the mound of ripe fruits from escaping. "Once Rosealise teaches me how to weave some baskets, we can fill a couple dozen. Stop looking so glum. She knows how to make scones."

Mael eyed the Englishwoman.

"Rather like bannocks," she explained.

"With milk and eggs and I might attempt a flummery, too."

"Wait, why do you look like you did right before we found the waterfall room?" Jenna asked her husband.

"Edane opened the mound in the forest," Domnall told her. "'Tis filled with cloth and weapons and goods. 'Twould seem 'tis possessions taken from travelers attacked here."

"Attacked," Rosealise whispered. Seeds spilled to the ground as she stared at the chieftain, her gaze blank. "They shot my driver, and the horses bolted. The coach overturned." She made a harsh sound, covering her mouth with her hand, and then went very still. "I think I must go inside now."

Chapter Eleven

IN THE DEPTHS of the tunnel Danar pitted his considerable bulk against the collapsed stone again and again before staggering back. Dark blood streaked down the side of his face as he regarded Iolar.

"It does not open, my prince."

"Get out of my way."

Summoning the power that had elevated him to rule, Iolar unleashed its full fury, until a white, crackling wall of ice stretched out before him. He struck it with his fist, and the ice shattered, collapsing around his legs.

Beyond it the stone rubble remained in place.

Iolar slapped his claws against the stone, probing it with his magic. Through it he could no longer feel the energy of the underworld, which meant the long passage leading to it had also been completely filled in. But it could not be, for they had used this very same gate only a few hours past.

While they had been hunting souls to cull, someone had come here and sealed off the passage.

"Who did this?" He turned on his *deamhanan*, all of whom dropped to their knees and bowed their heads. *"Who?"*

None of the Sluath moved or spoke.

Had he iron at hand, Iolar would have killed them all. "I'll spare the life of the *deamhan* responsible, but only if he makes himself known to me. *Now.*"

Again, the silence was broken only by the faint echo of his voice.

Kicking demons out of his path, Iolar strode out of the cave. The clear skies that greeted him made him bellow his rage, for without a storm he could not take wing. That meant walking to another entrance they could use. Walking, as if he were no more than mortal scum. Behind him the sounds of squabbling came with the thuds of blows, which quickly grew loud as the Sluath began fighting each other.

"Meirneal," he shouted over the din.

The diminutive *deamhan* rushed out of the cave and fell before Iolar face-down in the dirt. "I would never betray you, my prince, never. You must believe—"

"Stop your prattling." He seized Meirneal's curly head and dragged him up to his eye level. For all his prettiness the sight of his fear most gratified the prince. "Where is the nearest entrance we may use?"

His cherubic lips trembled. "There are no more left open, my prince."

Iolar had not experienced this degree of surprise since long ago learning that the rebels had escaped. He found it immensely unpleasant.

"If you're jesting with me, you little fiend, I will use your bones as my toothpicks."

"They are all sealed, my prince," Meirneal whispered. "Like this one." His eyes shifted toward the cave. "Attend our prince, you blighted scum," he called out.

Iolar's most trusted *deamhanan* staggered out of the cave and fell to their knees.

"All of the gates are like this?" he demanded.

"We would have told you sooner, my prince." A battered Clamhan crawled over to them, and tugged down his broken skull mask. "We did not wish to trouble you."

Iolar dropped the small *deamhan*. The glamour cloaking his lieutenants had begun to bulge in odd places as the souls they had devoured fought to free themselves. There was a similar roiling in his own belly and chest.

"If we cannot return to the underworld," he said, using his pleasantest tone, "we cannot feed on our prey, or contain them. They will escape us. Our slaves below will die." As the *deamhanan* stared up at him the air became filled with snow and he shouted, "Have you fools no understanding of what you have done?"

"We disappointed you, Prince Iolar." Seabhag rose from his knees and tottered forward. His shifting form went from a buxom female to that of an old crone and back again. "But we remain loyal to you, as always. This had to be the work of the traitor who freed the rebels and stole your treasure."

"You are as quick to point the finger of blame as you are to swear fealty," Iolar said. "Is there nothing you can offer me but excuses and sniveling?"

He heard a snicker that drew his gaze to one of the newer *deamhanan*. He could not recall the name he had taken, but he had barely survived the change. Even as the prince watched, a culled soul escaped the newling's lips to fade on the wind.

Iolar crooked a claw at the now-pale deamhan. "You, come to me."

The Sluath rose and crept closer, stopping just beyond the prince's reach. "'Twere no' I what done this to ye, milord."

"You still speak like a fucking mortal." He cocked his head, aware that Seabhag and Meirneal were quickly moving away now. They still had some value to him, so he ignored their cowering. "Have we taught you nothing of what it means to be Sluath?"

The newling made as if to reply, had a bright moment, and instead clamped his mouth shut.

"I speak of the nobility of our kind, and the dignity with which we conduct ourselves.

All that we have learned through traveling the ages and culling the weakest from mortal kind. We are the most powerful beings in creation, the embodiment of carnal glory, and yet you dare babble at me like some dirt-wallowing peasant." He tasted the thin tendrils of the *deamhan's* fear. "What is your name?"

The deamhan started to reply, and then gasped as a shaft of ice impaled him through the gut. As black blood poured from the wound, he shook his head frantically.

"No, please, milord—my prince," he begged. "My name 'tis Frew. I'll learn to do right, to speak as the others." He choked as a second soul escaped him. "Please, I wish to live."

"You should have thought of that before you flapped your lips, Frew." Iolar approached him, twisting the shaft that connected his arm with the *deamhan's* gut. He created a second with his other. "But do beg me again for your life. Persuade me why I should spare it. Perhaps mention what value, if any, you have to me."

"I ken, I know…what…what…"

A liquid gurgle cut off Frew's voice as the

prince rammed the second ice shaft through his broad neck. Using the shafts like shears, Iolar tore the *deamhan's* body apart, shaking off the ice and the torn carcass. The remaining souls contained by Frew's form burst from the remains and vanished. The body then began to revert back to what it had been before attaining demonic power, curling up and shrinking into a twisted ruin.

Iolar went to perch on a rock and watch the skies. After a long interval Danar came to stand beside him. He could hear the others setting fire to Frew's remains and speaking quietly among themselves. His anger faded beneath the dismal prospect of being trapped in the mortal realm. It was no coincidence that all the gates had been sealed while he'd been here. Nothing like this had ever been done to him, and he wanted to know why.

"My prince," Danar said, his tone as careful as his expression.

"If you try to placate me now," the prince said, "I shall rip off your face with a blunt claw."

"I must speak to the necessities of our situation," his second said. "We need a place to dwell until such time as we may return to the underworld. Horses as well, so we might travel quickly. Then we will have time to find the bastard responsible for this sabotage and gut him by inches as he roasts over a fire."

Idly curious, Iolar regarded the big *deamhan*. In Danar's eyes was the ever-present respect, but no true fear. He looked hungry, but he had the sort of appetite that would never be satiated.

"What were you before you came to the Sluath?"

Danar's mouth curled on one side. "A barbarian king. I set fire to great cities, and plundered their riches, and slaughtered more men than could be counted. I then raped their women, and enslaved them and their children."

"Ah. That's probably why I never want to disembowel you." He regarded the horizon. "Send scouts to the highest ground to look for suitable caves. If we can't reopen any of the gates, then we will create one."

Doubt flickered across the Sluath's face. "It's been thousands of years since the first of our kind fashioned them, my prince. None that knew how it's done are…left."

Iolar approved of his cautious wording. Being reminded that he had assassinated them all in order to take the throne never bettered his mood.

"Our pet druid may prove useful in that regard. Find him."

Chapter Twelve

THE STRANGE TRANCE Rosealise experienced in the garden was not what had made her weak and trembling, but she kept the true cause of her fear to herself. To reveal it would distress her friends, who would wish to help. She knew nothing could be done for her now. It also gave her reason to insist Jenna leave her and go with her husband to inspect what might be salvaged from the hidden cache.

"I will have a rest in my room, and later help you sort what the men bring back," she promised. Forcing a smile, she turned to Mael but kept from touching him. "You should go with them."

The seneschal first accompanied her to her chamber, where he removed his tartan and wrapped it around her.

"You yet shake," he said when she tried to refuse it. "And you're as pale as snow. 'Tis the shock of recalling the attack."

"I don't, really," she admitted. "What I said came purely in response to Domnall's revelation. Simply words. I have no true memory of what occurred." What had made her feel as if she'd frozen inside threatened to overwhelm her now. "I am very tired."

He led her into the room. "You've a headache again, I'll wager."

"I'm becoming quite the invalid." She went to sit down on her bed, wriggling a little as the evergreen branches shifted under her. If he didn't leave soon, she would expose her secret. "Go and join the others, please, if you wish." And now she would have to lie again. "I will soon recover, I promise you."

Mael lingered for another moment before he nodded and left. Rosealise lay down on the furs and glanced at the hand she'd used to cover her mouth in the garden. She then turned her face into her pillow to muffle the sound before she released the cough she'd been holding back. It led to another, and more, until she tasted a coppery wetness.

She lifted her face from the pillow to stare at the patches of wet crimson now staining the sacking. The same stained her palm. The brief, knife-like pain in her chest when she'd spilled the seeds had disappeared. Yet the location of the pain and the blood confirmed her suspicions, and wrote what would rule the last chapter of her life.

Consumption.

Rosealise drew Mael's tartan tightly around her and turned the pillow over to hide the stains. How she recognized the deadly affliction was lost along with her memories, but she knew its effects and progress. Nothing could be done to stop it. She would slowly decline from her present state to a pale, feverish infirmity plagued by a worsening, liquid cough. Her lungs would fill slowly, diminishing her until she could no longer rise from her bed. In the end a gradual suffocation would snuff out her life.

There could be only one explanation for her vast knowledge: *I watched someone die of this.* Judging by the sorrow that came with the understanding of the illness, someone she had loved dearly.

So I will die the same.

It seemed she had some time left. The blood that had come from her coughing appeared bright red and had been scant. She would have to tell Mael, for she had kissed him. Such intimate contact put him at risk of catching her dreadful disease. Absolutely there would be no more kissing, but not out of deference to a lover she couldn't remember.

My dear friend. Rosealise rolled onto her back and stared up at the thatched boughs over her. *Now I may never again feel your embrace.*

Forcing herself to get up, she used water from a skin Jenna had given her to wash her hands and face, blotting them with the edge of her borrowed tunic. It was then she noticed the edge of something pale protruding from a gap between two stones in the wall beside her bed. Hoping it wasn't a bone, she reached down to retrieve it. Her fingers stilled as she touched the rolled edge, which felt like stiff paper. It took some prying to work it out of the stones, but once she did she saw it was a flattened scroll. Carefully she opened it, and carried it over to the window slit to better look at the dense markings.

It appeared to be a map. The drawing appeared very recent, and yet in a style quite archaic. It showed a sprawling stone structure of many levels, each crammed with tiny details. Rectangles drawn in dozens of spots over the building had been scraped clean and filled with tiny pictures: rigid-looking warriors with fuzzy heads, two frothing waterfalls, and gems so beautifully rendered their ink seemed to glitter. She saw no citation, legend or scale indicator, but a small triangle at the bottom seemed to indicate the north direction.

Only when she spotted the maze next to the structure did she realize what the map depicted: Dun Chaill.

"By my honor," she murmured.

Rosealise turned over the parchment but the back had been left unmarked. She then crouched down to examine the stones where it had been left. She couldn't fathom why anyone would attempt to hide the scroll in such a spot. Her chamber offered far more suitable areas for concealment.

Someone wanted me to find it.

Faint scratches on the edges of the stones suggested someone had chipped away at this spot —and quite recently, judging by the sharp condition of the edges. When she touched a fingertip to the gap to gauge its depth a flick of light passed through the rock, which then dissolved.

Backing away, Rosealise watched as more flickerings spread, and an arch-shaped portion of the stone wall disappeared, engulfing her in a cloud of dust. She coughed in earnest now, which stabbed another dagger of pain into her breast. Clutching the scroll she stumbled to her bed, but lack of air drove her to her knees.

The door to her chamber flung open, and Mael rushed in to lift her into his arms.

"No," she gasped. The coughing spasm ended, but she still turned her face away from him. "You must not..." She stopped and gulped some air.

"I couldnae leave you here alone, thank the Gods." Carefully he placed her on the bed, retrieving the waterskin to bring it to her, and then froze. "Rosealise, 'tis blood on your lips."

Unable to speak of it, she met his gaze. From the dread in his expression Mael also knew the cause. He propped her up with his arm and gave her some sips from the water-skin spout. The coughing finally abated, allowing her to catch her breath.

"I do beg your pardon," Rosealise murmured, swallowing against the rawness in her throat. "I'd hoped I was wrong, but in the garden I left blood on my hand, and I knew then what afflicted me."

His jaw tightened. "I'll fetch Edane. We saw the white plague many times as lads, and he kens much of healing potions—"

"Nothing he can do will cure me." She tried to smile. "You've been very brave, Seneschal, but you must leave me now. Do tell the others not to come too close now. I would not condemn anyone else to my fate."

Mael looked away, and then saw the arch that had appeared in the wall.

"By the Gods."

"I neglected to mention," Rosealise said,

"that I believe I've found another magical trap, and this."

She held out the scroll, but he was already up and approaching the arch. She pushed herself off the bed, reaching for his hand.

Everything around them grew dazzling white, and Mael and the room vanished.

Chapter Thirteen

ROSEALISE SAT SILENTLY in the silken cage of her slave cell, her gaze fixed on the far wall. The short, diaphanous peignoir she wore fluttered with every breath she took, as if meaning to ceaselessly taunt her. She ignored how deplorably she had been clad, in the same way she'd disregarded every other unpleasant aspect of her captivity.

Soon it would end, by escape or by death. Both seemed the same to her now.

She wished she could see through the stone to what lay beyond it. The dreadful terrors that abounded here didn't frighten her as much as the atrocious creatures who reveled in them. The small, childlike monster that had stolen her from her time had proven especially vicious. Yet her fear centered not on her fate, but that of the gentle titan who shared her cell. Just after they had awakened the Sluath had come for him, leaving her to wait alone for his return. Here there was no day or night, only endless stretches of idle time, each passing hour dragging slower than the last.

Mael, what have they done with you?

Battling her own dread had become a daily trial. The Pritani hunter had protected her almost from the moment she'd been dragged into this infernal netherworld. Without him she'd be at the mercy of the demons, who relished tormenting their slaves. Lately she had lived for every moment spent with Mael. Thinking of him always helped hold back the terror lurking in her heart, for he had become her one, unbreakable grip on hope. Now she had another reason to live, but it would tear them apart.

What would you do to see him free? That was the question she constantly put to herself. The answer had never wavered, nor would it now. *Anything, anything at all.*

The wall finally dissolved into a shower of

light, and Mael staggered into the chamber. His garments hung in shreds from his bloodied body, attesting to the violence he'd endured. Rosealise hurried over to him, tucking herself under his arm as she helped him over to a divan. He smelled of sweat and death, and sand caked his boots.

They put him back in the arena.

The Sluath took great delight in making slaves fight each other, Mael had told her, but he wouldn't describe exactly what happened during those bouts. Her imagination and his appearance made that only too plain.

"No, don't move," Rosealise told him as she tore a sleeve from her gown. "You're badly injured."

"'Tisnae my blood, lass." He took the sleeve from her and used it to wipe the gore from his face. "That wee fiend wants naught but to see me a wet smear on the sands, the facking ghoul. If only I might put him to my blade."

"They'd kill you if you tried." She sat down beside him, and took one of his bruised hands in hers. "Oh, blazes. Did Meirneal force you to fight one of your friends?"

"'Twas a Roman," Mael said but his shoulders hunched, and he wouldn't look at her. "He'd gone mad from the torments, so mayhap 'tis merciful that I ended him. Gods help me, but I cannae feel 'twas."

"This was their doing," Rosealise told him, "not yours." She brought his hand to her heart, and leaned close to put her lips next to his ear. "Jenna got word to me. All is prepared for the next culling feast."

His arms came around her, and Mael held her for a long moment before he sighed.

"Now ye shall need a bathe," he said. "Go on, lass. I'll wait."

"You'll do no such thing." Rising to her feet, she tugged on his hand and led him over to the sunken spring pool they used for bathing. When he started to protest, she pressed a finger against his lips. "They brought me here to serve you, remember? Yet you always attend to me. Allow me to do this for you."

Rosealise helped him remove the tattered remains of his clothing before she went to work with the soap. Her hands lingered and stroked him as she washed away the blood from his flesh. She didn't care how wanton that made her. In a few days all of this would be decided, but she couldn't bear the thought of what might happen to him.

We have a few more nights before the feast.

After she rinsed away the soap with a bucket Mael stepped down into the pool, sinking to his shoulders and sighing as the steaming water engulfed him. His expression remained defeated, however, until Rosealise shrugged out of her ruined peignoir and slipped into the pool with him.

The luxury of immersing herself in the spring's heat paled beside the wicked delight of being unclothed with him. Society would have soundly condemned her as a trollop for such behavior. Here it seemed the most loving gift she could offer her friend.

Not my friend. My lover.

"I'd keep my vow to ye, lass," Mael told her, his big hands gripping her waist when she moved closer. "But ye're all the beauty I ken in this foul place, and I'm no' made of stone."

"I do recall how you promised that you wouldn't bed me, just after I swore never to kiss you." Rosealise pressed her body to his, gasping a little as his thick erection did the same between her thighs. "We're not in the bed now, my titan, and I will happily forego the kisses."

"You ken what I meant," he argued, and yet stroked his palms up along her back. "I'll no' fack ye. 'Tis what they want."

"I agree." Filled with tenderness, she pressed her cheek to his. "You should instead indulge my passion for you."

The water darkened around them, and then the strange blue-white fires in the braziers and hearth extinguished. Suddenly the cell vanished, and all around her appeared feathery ferns bathed in sunlight. Tall white flowers with golden hearts rose from the thick carpet of fronds, their petals glistening with remnant dew. The air smelled of ripe fruit, and when she glanced up, she saw why. Gray-green vines heavily laden with silvered blue grapes nearly covered the weathered stone walls of the roofless chamber.

A tendril of breeze from above brought downy seeds with it, spangling the air.

Being wrenched from that erotic vision to this enchanting garden room made Rosealise

feel giddy and disoriented, but the warmth
beside her made her turn her head. Mael, his
eyes filled with disbelief, lay next to her in the
ferns. As the sun-warmed air rushed over
them she saw the blood trickling down from a
gash on his brow. More stained the edge of a
stone by his head.

"You're hurt," she cried out, reaching for
his wound.

༄༅༅

MAEL FELT the blood stop flowing and the raw
edges puckering as they shrank, even as
Rosealise made to press her fingers against his
gash. Her eyes widened, and her hand stilled
an inch from his face.

"How can you heal so swiftly?"

"I ever do." He wiped the blood from his
brow. Belatedly he realized their bodies were
touching, but before he could break the
contact, he told her the rest. "Naught may
sicken me, or cause me grow older. No matter
how grave, my wounds mend as you now see.
'Tis made me immortal."

She peered at him, but her gray eyes

seemed unfocused. "The Sluath did this to you?"

"I dinnae recall it, but we ken that the demons move through time," Mael said. "They took us from the first century, but we escaped and awoke in the second. 'Tis been twelve centuries since the Mag Raith escaped the underworld."

"That is the truth?" When he nodded, she made an odd sound. "Oh, my dear friend. I cannot think of what to say."

He took hold of her hand, and pressed a kiss to her palm. "Say 'twillnae make you fear me."

Rosealise's lips curved. "I could never be afraid of you, Seneschal. Not after how we were together in the underworld."

"Do you remember when I came from the arena?" he asked, recalling his own vision.

Rosealise described what she called a dream of him, which matched in every detail what he had seen. She seemed unaware that she had wedged herself against him as she had in the spring pool, so that her sex closely nestled against his. Mael knew it to be unseemly, but he wouldn't have moved away if his life had depended on it.

"So, you see, it all makes sense now," she said at last. "What I know of love you taught me. The dream proves it."

"'Twasnae a dream but a memory shared. I saw the same before I awoke here." The ferns rustled around them as he started to rise, but Rosealise clung to him. "My lady, we must find our way out. 'Tisnae wise to linger." His head had already begun to spin with heat and desire for her, and if his cock swelled any larger, he'd disgrace himself.

"I agree. Absolutely imprudent." A laugh slipped from her as she drew him back down beside her. "No wonder you seemed so familiar to me." She ran her hands over his chest and arms, her eyes sparkling with reckless joy. "Since the moment I fell into the maze I knew you. I only wish I could remember more of you—of us, together as we were."

"'Tis enough that we ken." Before he could think Mael wrapped his arms around her, pressing her against the full length of him. "I reckon 'tis why I've longed for you every night since you came. To wake and wish you in my bed, to share the quiet hour before the day begins."

"I should be shocked, but I am not." Rosealise released a slow, sensual sound. "What would you share with me, my titan?"

"My body. My heart. Everything I've to give." Mael looked all over her face. He could feel her pebbling nipples through the wool of his tunic now. Gods, but he wanted her. "And you'd do the same."

"As I'd do now," she murmured, rubbing the outside of his thigh with the inside of her own. "If you would kindly disrobe me first. I long to feel your hands on my skin."

"Like so?"

Mael slipped his fingers under the edge of her tunic, sliding his palm over her bare belly and up to her throbbing breast.

When the roughness of his hand covered her mound Rosealise arched her back. "Oh, dear Mael. I feel so ripe and hot."

"Aye, and you look it." He massaged her, his fingers tracing and then gently squeezing her puckered nipple. Her skin moved under his touch like mist made flesh. "I want to see you naked again."

Rosealise suddenly pulled up her tunic, baring herself to his gaze. "I think if you only look, I would weep. Oh."

He put his mouth to her breast, caressing her nipple with his lips before taking it into his mouth. She tasted so sweet he groaned, and Rosealise answered him with a softer sound of delight. She clasped him with her thighs, and shifted onto her back, rolling her shoulders as if inviting him to adore her other mound. In another moment he braced himself over her, his mouth ravishing her curves and tormenting her peaks until she gripped his hair and pushed her hips against his.

She was ready and eager and yet everything that felt so good also felt wrong.

Mael took his mouth from her. He shook his head, trying to clear away the fog clouding his mind.

"You're a lady. I'd never—"

"But you have. We shared the memory of it." Rosealise laughed like an excited bairn, and then stopped and frowned. "How strange. I never giggle." She stroked the back of his neck. "But no matter. I admit, I cannot offer you a bathe here. Oh, Mael, I don't wish to use my power, but I'm so fraught with wanting you."

"Your eyes, they've gone almost black." He stared down at her until something emerged from his muddled thoughts: the memory of Fargas after a long night of drinking. "Fack the Gods." He pushed himself up and tugged her into a sitting position. "We must escape this trap now, my lady, before we become too addled."

"Must we this very moment?" Rosealise took a petal that had caught in his hair and drew the soft edge across his lips. "I'd much rather stay and reacquaint you with my naked-ness, if that is your wish."

"I want naught else, but no' if it costs our lives." He lifted her up with him, holding her upright as he took in the chamber again. The air had grown heavy, sweet, and hazy. Tiny threads of silver that matched those covering the fruit hanging from the walls floated thick around them. "'Tis the grapes. Every breath tastes of wine. 'Tis making us drunk."

"I have no memory of ever indulging in spirits," Rosealise told him, and then rubbed at her face. "I think you are correct. I can no longer feel my nose. Do you see the arch?"

"Aye."

Mael used the last of his will to swing her up over his shoulder and staggered toward one of the walls.

"You needn't hurry," she said. "Do you know, upside-down this chamber looks like a vineyard roofed with a garden. It's so charming. If you wish to, we could linger a few more minutes, surely–"

Mael got to the arch and stepped through it. A shimmer of light burst over them, and the garden chamber vanished. Back in her chamber again, he lowered her to her feet, and tugged her tunic back down over her breasts.

Rosealise's hand went to her throat as the dazed expression cleared from her face.

"Forgive me–" he said, just as she gasped, "I'm so sorry–"

They both lapsed into silence.

Mael glanced at the wall but it looked as it had before they'd gone through it. Remembering the garden, Mael thought of his sire. He saw Fargas sprawling on the floor of his *broch*, snoring off another night of swilling ale and beating his mate and daughters. Suddenly he understood the man as he never before had, and it disgusted him.

"Forgive me, my lady." Mael started for the door.

"No, don't go away," Rosealise said, catching his arm. When her power stopped him, she yanked back her hand. "I didn't mean to control you. Of course, you can leave."

"Aye." Mael said, turning to face her. To see the distress on her lovely face piled shame atop his self-loathing. "I must, else I'd never leave you again."

"I'd never want you to." She held up her hands, as if to show him that she wasn't touching him. "Please, Mael, do as you truly wish."

Chapter Fourteen

GALAN RODE THE last surge of the storm across the western midlands, his healed wings effortlessly gliding through the rough air. Now he understood the Sluath's contempt for grounddwelling mortals, for flying proved so thrilling he never wished to again land on his feet. The strange magic of the wings, however, disappeared as soon as the skies cleared. Compelled to circle down until his boots touched the earth, he flexed his shoulders to fold the goldtipped white feathers into a hump that he concealed with a murmured body ward spell.

The muddy ground squelched under his footsteps as he strode across the glen. Soon he

would have to report to Prince Iolar that he
had been unable to locate the Mag Raith.

*I should return to the Moss Dapple and question
those facking fools. Domnall may have confided in one
of them.*

As he reached the edge of the glen Galan
saw a female and stopped in his tracks. The
plump-cheeked dairy maid sat on a horse
outside the shepherd's shelter he had been
using. Her coy expression made his upper
lip curl.

"You'll find no drovers here to trifle with,
slut. Begone with you."

"I never cared for drovers in my trifle. Too
stringy." The maid's body shifted to that of a
huge, scarred Norse warrior. "Iolar would
make use of you now, you fatuous tree-licker,
or I'd happily make you my next meal."

The demon's angry bitterness had nothing
to do with him, so Galan kept his own expression neutral. "What does he wish me to do?"

"He'll tell you." The Norseman shifted
into a wizened druidess, who scratched under
her pendulous breasts. "Get your mount."

They rode from the glen up into the highlands, where Seabhag led him to the spot

where Iolar had created his wings. Glancing down at the dark spatters that still stained the ground, Galan dismounted. Iolar and Danar emerged from the cave along with a dozen angry-looking demons, who promptly encircled him. Galan bowed deeply, but before he could speak Seabhag seized him by the back of the neck and shoved him down on his knees.

"Here I think is the traitor, my prince," the demon said, driving the tips of his claws into Galan's flesh. "He knew we use the caves. No other has reason to betray us."

"With your power augmenting his magic," Meirneal said, excitement sharpening his cherubic features, "he could easily seal off the gates to the underworld."

Danar made a disgusted sound. "The tree-worshipper only discovered our existence recently. The other gates were sealed long before that."

"You know how long these inviolate fuckers carry their memories," Seabhag said, crouching down as his face shifted into a nightmare of twisted flesh. "You knew of us in a former life, didn't you, worm? Confess and reopen the gate, and I will kill you quickly."

To respond in any manner would only end his life, Galan suspected, so he deliberately glanced past the monstrous visage. "You summoned me, my prince?"

"Release him, Seabhag," Iolar ordered and loomed over him, his godlike face set in a peevish scowl. "While we hunted, someone sealed our last gate to the underworld. Until it can be reopened, we remain trapped here."

"Permit me to behold the gate," Galan said carefully as he rose to his feet, "and I may sense the manner of magic used to seal it."

Iolar nodded, and led him into the cave. The tunnel he took abruptly ended in a wall of stone that appeared as ancient as the rest of the rock faces around it.

"Well?" the prince demanded.

Galan lifted his hands, holding them an inch from the stone, and murmured a simple revelation spell. Dark blue lines rayed out from beneath his palms, spreading and curving until they formed an archway. The tunnel echoed with the sound of grating rocks as the wall expanded another inch out, sprouting new angles and outcroppings as the dark light grew more intense.

The backlash of the power left in place burned Galan's palms, and he took several steps back and shielded the prince with his own body. As soon as he moved away the arch of light quickly faded, and the rock face stopped expanding.

"'Twasnae done by druid magic," he said, turning to face Iolar. "Nor that of the Sluath. 'Tis mortal magic, very ancient."

"No, no, no," the prince said. "Our gates kill any mortal who attempts to pass through them."

"Mayhap they didnae have to enter the gate to work this magic," Galan said. "Or their power protected them. A powerful Pritani enlisting the aid of a battle spirit, or the Gods themselves, might do such. Only the one who sealed it may remove the spell."

"Pritani." Iolar struck the side of the tunnel with a swipe of his claws, sending a shower of sparks to bounce around Galan's boots. "Those fucking rebels could not have done this alone."

Galan seized on the chance to enhance the

prince's suspicions and deflect blame from himself. "Before the Mag Raith left the mortal realm their tribe trained Edane, the archer, to serve as shaman. Mayhap one of your kind told him how 'twas to be done." He gestured toward the cave entrance. "I shall search the area for tracks or other trace of their passage."

"Take the *deamhanan* with you," Iolar ordered. The prince looked over as the four demons who served as his lieutenants approached. "You useless idiots will find out who among us is the traitor or I will assume it was all of you."

Chapter Fifteen

ROSEALISE'S HANDS FELL as she watched Mael back away from her. He looked as if he were in torment, until his shoulder touched the door. He turned and yanked it open.

"We cannae stay here," he said, jutting his chin toward the wall where the arch had appeared. He extended his hand.

He wasn't leaving her. Her heart filled with such jubilation she thought it might burst from her body. She took his hand and he led her into his chamber. Once inside he moved the bolt bar, slipping it into the catch.

"Your head's clear?" he asked her, his tone soft but intent as he took a step toward her. "You ken in truth what you're asking of me?"

"Entirely." She moved toward him now, because to be apart from him had become suddenly and absolutely unbearable. To speak honestly made her tremble, for it seemed so blunt and unladylike, but she could no longer deny her desires, either. "I want what we had in that terrible place, Mael. What we gave to each other in those wretched times. The beauty and grace that we found together."

By that moment only scant inches separated them, and still he did not put his hands on her. This close his strong, broad body seemed especially massive, and as still as if hewn from stone. His scent had grown intense, as if fire surrounded them in a forest ablaze. Her own blended with it in the space between them, and he breathed in deeply before he lifted his fingers to her cheek.

"The beauty and grace, 'tis all yours." He traced her cheekbone and jaw line. "As a priceless jewel you are, my *jem*, and I'm as a lad with his first lass."

It didn't surprise her to feel the slight tremor from the fingertips dancing over her skin. It matched the frantic pounding of her heart.

"I too feel a little fraught. Any word I may say now could force you to act against your will."

He touched his mouth to her brow before he looked into her eyes. "Naught you want shall I ever deny you. I'm yours."

Rosealise took hold of his hands, and brought them to the hem of her tunic. "I wish to be wholly naked with you again, as we were in the pool." Together they lifted the garment over her head, baring her to the waist. Then she released her hair from its twist.

Mael brushed her hair back from her face and shoulders, and looked down at her heaving breasts for a long moment. "I'd feel all of your lovely body on mine."

In the same manner they undressed each other. Once they stood naked the heat of their bodies dispelled the last of Rosealise's unsteady nerves. How could she fear such a man, when every tough bulge and broad expanse of his frame made her fingers and lips tingle so madly? She eliminated the last gap between them, and the paleness of her thin skin against his darker, harder flesh made her feel beyond elated.

"Jenna and Domnall share the same skin-work," he murmured. "Yours looks the reflection of my own." He touched her thigh, and caught his breath as he met her gaze. "Do you feel that, inside you?"

Rosealise nodded, her lashes lowering as the sparkling exhilaration raced through her skin. "I feel the same each time you come close to me."

"I hate that they branded you," Mael said as he moved his hand along the glyphs. "But 'tis what connects us, I reckon."

"There is more than that," she chided. "You are as kind as you are strong, and I daresay you've saved me again and again. But simply to be with you has become my obsession. I cannot enter a room without looking first for you. If you are not there, I listen for your voice."

His mouth hitched. "'Tis the same for me."

"I am torn now," she murmured, and stroked her hands up his arms before twining her fingers behind his neck. "I long to caress you, and yet I think if you do not soon embrace me I might—"

Mael didn't let her finish. His mouth took hers. The moment she gasped he put his tongue between her lips in the most shocking fashion. Then his taste suffused her, and the sensual stroking of his tongue against hers sent a weighty surge of aching sensation down into her belly. Surely, she had never experienced such rampaging hunger as this, and the moan that ended the kiss ignited a frenzied clutch of hands and shifting of hips for them both.

"I'd take you to my bed," he said, his voice so low and hard it sounded like a threat. "And come between your thighs, and have you with my cock as I kiss and touch you."

"You put me to blush." Rosealise put her cheek against his so he could feel the color flooding her face. "I wish only that your bed stood closer."

Mael picked her up and rushed with her across the chamber, rolling to his back on the bed. He planted her atop him, just as they had been that first time in the maze. Only now he gazed up at her, his bejeweled eyes dark and gleaming.

"Gods, but to look upon you thus," he said lowly. "To hold you to me, and ken you'll be mine. 'Tis every loveliness dreamed." He touched her face, and then slowly slid his hand down, boldly stroking her breast and her belly before gripping her thigh. "I wish to wake, my beautiful *jem*, as we are now, and no' ever sleep again."

"Then I must endeavor to keep you awake." She clasped his hips with her knees, rising to put her throbbing sex against the broad column of his. Now she understood why she had become awash and full of soft heat. Her body wanted him as much as she did. It was open and ready for the thick, heavy shaft that pulsed against her. "Perhaps I should indulge your passion for me."

Bending until she could brazenly press her lips to his, Rosealise kissed him. Did she dare to do so as he had her? She attempted it, smiling against his mouth as he groaned into hers.

The chamber upended as Mael flipped with her, tucking her under his huge frame and surging between her legs. He held the kiss a moment longer, until the whimper of need that spilled from her throat made him reach between their bodies. She moaned with relief as he guided his rampant erection to her, notching the smooth bulb of his cockhead between her folds.

"Yes, that is what I wish," Rosealise told him, lifting her hips as he pushed into her softness. "More and more and more of you, yes, please."

"So you shall have," he said, bracing himself over her.

Mael's girth stretched her around him as he sank with one long, luxurious stroke into her body. Whatever they had shared in the past had to pale beside this joining, this merging. His penetration made her feel as if she bloomed around him, engulfing and clasping him so tenderly. Kisses were but preparation for this, for her quim taking his steely male length so deeply and perfectly.

At last their body hair curled as snugly as they fit together, and Rosealise pressed her hand against his chest. His pulse thudded hard and heavy and sure, and she could feel it inside her as well as under her palm.

"I've captured the heart of you, my titan," she whispered to him, and brought his hand to her left breast. "Now, take mine."

All the wonder of Rosealise's vision became her world as Mael moved over her. Between her legs his shaft retreated and returned, filling her so exquisitely she writhed around him. He made her a tempest into which he drove, his muscles bulging and flexing, until her body became his to pleasure. She moved with him, mindless and greedy for more, her lips caressing his neck, his shoulder, his jaw. The midnight fire of his scent filled her, spreading warmth over the dazzling streaks of sensation as he forged in and out.

Rosealise clutched his arms as something else welled up inside her. It was as huge as him, as inescapable and possessing as his need. She might have cried out for fear of it, but she knew this, just as she knew him. Instead she surrendered to it, tears spilling from her lashes as it overcame her, and her body stretched and shivered one last moment before the bliss smashed through her.

"Aye, my *jem*, aye," Mael said, his voice falling to a rough growl as his cock pumped harder and deeper. "'Tis lovely, you're lovely, that's all I wish, to make you come."

As the shattering sensations pulsed

through Rosealise she felt as if she might dissolve into a flood of pleasure and puddle beneath him. How could one survive such utter possession of the senses? *To know it again,* she answered herself, and looked up at the fierce satisfaction in his dark eyes. He had conquered her will, and still moved in her, his hard shaft slow and deliberate as he stroked her through the last of the tremors.

"You have had your way with me again, you wicked man," Rosealise said, and curled her leg around the back of his. She rolled with him, tightening her quim to keep his weighty cock nestled deep as she straddled him. "Now, to be fair, I should have mine."

Placing her hands on his wide shoulders, she lifted herself. Just as the slick length of his shaft would have left her, she impaled herself on him. Using the muscles she had just discovered, she then clenched his hard length. Instinct moved her in a small, leisurely whirl about him.

Mael flinched as if she'd struck him, and grabbed hold of her hips. A hungry smile bared his teeth. "Again."

"So, I can have you in something of the

same manner. How gratifying." She eased her clenching hold and rose again, sliding back down to take every stiff inch inside herself. "I'd make you shake and groan, as you did to me just now. I wish to feel your senses roil and quake as well." As she spoke, she worked her quim over him, circling slowly as she clasped, until her body became a glove and a caress all at once. "I want to make you come for me, inside me, all over me."

Her words seemed to inflame his passions as much as her ministrations. He stared up at her, an unending groan rumbling from his chest. His big hands slid around to grip her bottom, urging her rhythm until she rode him with unrestrained vigor.

"I'd soon fill you with my seed," he murmured, squeezing her bouncing buttocks with unabashed lust. "So much awaits 'twill pour from you like a secret rain."

The carnal promise sent a shiver of new need through her.

"That will be welcome." Rosealise lowered herself so that the hard peak of her breast just grazed his mouth. "I will wear you as my new perfume. Oh." As he latched onto her and began to suck, she shivered around him, and his body tensed beneath her. "Mael, come to me now."

He muttered something against her nipple, and then thrust her down onto his cock just as the first stream erupted from it. Rosealise squeezed his shaft again, feeling her own desires swelling with him. As he pumped long, thick spurts into her core, the potent warmth and wetness triggered another burst inside her. The climax grew softer and longer as it matched the pulsating wildness of his.

Gently Mael brought her down to cradle her against the billowing swell of his chest, and ran his hand over her curls. "What want you now, lass?"

Though true hope she'd never again know, with every breath she took Rosealise felt her contentment grow deeper.

"The remainder of my days with you, Seneschal."

Chapter Sixteen

AS THE SUN sank into the violet twilight horizon, Edane used the sled Domnall had fashioned to bring another mound of tartans from the mound back to the keepe. It pleased him that they could salvage so much that they needed from the hoard, but he made sure to carefully inspect every plaid for stains and rends. He'd bring no reminder of a violent end into their home. Once he had added them to the pile stored in the old pantry, he went into the great hall to join his brothers and the women for the evening meal.

"We've enough wool now to fashion skirts and bodices for you lasses," he told Jenna, and then spied the map scroll spread out on the table. "Who drew this?"

"I found it in my room," Rosealise said, "along with a bespelled entry to a rather Bacchanalian trap."

She described what had happened so carefully Edane knew she'd left out many details. Mael also watched her closely, with the kind of deep affection showing in his eyes that came with a more physical bond. It seemed a natural match, although Edane felt sorrow for them both. Unless Dun Chaill's magic transformed Rosealise as it had Jenna, she would live out a mortal life leaving Mael behind to endure an eternity of loneliness.

"The map, 'twas another lure," Broden said flatly before he regarded the seneschal. "You shouldnae have taken the lady through the arch."

"I but approached it," Mael said and returned his angry glower. "The facking thing pulled us both in." He looked up at Edane. "'Twas the grapevines. They're enchanted."

"By the Gods," Edane muttered as he peered down at the scroll. Finally he recognized what it showed. "'Tis Dun Chaill, drawn like your architecture schemes, Jenna."

"True," she said, "but I really don't understand the *parti* of this place. Castles in this time were built as safeguards to keep an enemy and their siege weapons out. We know Dun Chaill was enlarged around a small fortress, but I've found no trace of any defensive measures, or quarters suitable for a garrison. Architecturally speaking, it doesn't make any sense."

"No' much about the place does," Domnall agreed. "Still, now that we have the map, mayhap we'll learn more."

"'Tis good, then," Edane declared but noticed the sober faces of the others. "Mael and the lady escaped the trap. Show some cheer, brothers."

"It's something else." Rosealise beckoned for him to sit down. "I've made a personal discovery that I've just now shared with the others. I have consumption, what you call the white plague." She tried to smile. "Not the happiest of news, I fear."

"Soot cleaning may cause a festering," he countered. He glanced at Mael, who had taken hold of the Englishwoman's hand.

"Surely you breathed in too much while cleaning the chimneys."

"'Twillnae hunt, Brother," the tracker said, his tone grim. "She coughs blood, and I saw enough of those stricken with it among our tribe to be sure."

"Fack the Gods," Broden said and abruptly rose and left the hall.

Domnall eyed Kiaran, who nodded before he went after him.

"We've some hope at least, my lady," the chieftain said softly.

"Jenna told me of the Sluath scout that ended her life, and how she awoke to immortality once inside the castle. Death may not be the end for me, either."

Edane eyed the chieftain's wife. "We're unsure of the magic that transformed her, and we cannae invoke it."

The Englishwoman nodded. "I am content to hope."

"In any case, Rosealise needs to keep up her strength," Jenna said, taking the map and rolling it up. "Let's have dinner."

The meal proved quiet and appetites dismal, thanks to the prevailing somber mood.

Edane discreetly studied the Englishwoman, noting the two subtle signs of her affliction: the patches of rosiness on her pale cheeks, and the shallow breaths she took to avoid coughing. When he had been in training the tribe had suffered two outbreaks of the white plague, although the shaman had always insisted on nursing the dying himself.

The plague hasnae ever caught me, lad. Dinnae tempt the Gods to heap more burden upon yer skinny shoulders.

At the time it had been a welcome reprieve from his always-onerous training. Now Edane realized how often the shaman had shielded him from such situations, and wondered why. He must have known that when Edane took his place he would have to attend to the sick.

A chill inched along his spine.

Or he reckoned I wouldnae ever become shaman.

"If you ken of a soothing tonic for Rosealise," Mael said to him, dragging him from his thoughts, "'twould aid her with the coughing bouts. Domnall and I must seal off Rosealise's room."

"I know now that you find such tasks

unpleasant, Edane," the Englishwoman said quickly. "Perhaps you could simply tell me how to prepare it, if you wish."

"'Tis naught for me to do it, my lady." He pushed away his half-eaten bowl of cold stew, glad to have a reason not to force it down. "I'll see to it at once."

In the kitchens Edane took mint, a jar of honey and a pot of fish oil from the shelves. It angered him to think of the Englishwoman being struck with such a cruel malady, but also instilled a strange guilt in him. For centuries he had lived like a god, unchanging and unwaveringly robust, seemingly forever spared the infirmities of age and sickness. Yet he had done nothing to earn such a tremendous boon.

He touched his chest, remembering the pain that had forced him to do the unthinkable.

I wished to die with the bow in my hands. Mayhap the old one was right, in that the Gods would see to it that I never shall.

When he emerged from the storage room, he found Rosealise waiting alone for him. To look upon her pale, pretty face made his anger shrink down to a tight misery.

"'Twill taste wretched, this tonic," he warned her as he carried everything over to the work table. "But 'tis good for the night, to permit you sleep. You must also seek to be outside in the sun each day when you may. The light aids the potion in clearing the lungs, although I cannae tell you why."

"I know that nothing will cure me. I believe I saw someone in my time die of this illness, someone I loved, I think." She joined him at the table. "Edane, what I'm not certain of is how long I may live with consumption. Can you advise me?"

"'Tis an affliction that grows slowly but steadily worse," he said as he tore the mint into shreds and dropped them into a stone mortar. "If you're coughing but a wee amount of blood…" At his glance she nodded. "Then you've still some time. You must guard against tiring and overwork, take the tonic nightly, and eat much greenery."

She stepped away from him. "I would not use my power, but I must know how much time is left to me. Please, sir, tell me."

Edane thought of the old shaman, and the terrible revelation he had made to him. Such truths could be as vicious as starved martens, but the pain faded quickly. Not to know proved a torment that never ended, and could drive a soul to take reckless measures.

He met her gaze. "None I've seen stricken with the bloody cough lived through a winter. The cold and the damage within that the plague caused, ever ended them."

"So, we could have summer and fall." A dreamy look stole over her face before she caught his look. "I apologize. Mael and I have become paramours, you see. Since I cannot make him sick, and I'd rather not sleep alone again in that room, I'll be staying in his chamber."

The softness of her voice confused him, for she spoke as if he'd given her a gift instead of the prediction of her death. "You'd be content with such a short life?"

"I feared it might only be weeks," Rosealise admitted. "Truly, any time we have left is precious to me."

BRODEN MOVED SILENTLY from where he had stood listening outside the kitchens. He knew Domnall needed his knowledge to contend with this newly-found trap. Then there was the map and what new secrets it might reveal. Yet if he looked upon Mael before his wrath cooled, he might stuff the scroll down the tracker's throat.

She's chosen him. As I reckoned.

Longing and envy had poisoned his mortal life, and Broden would have none of it. He'd made brothers of the Mag Raith hunters. These men had been the only family he'd ever known. He'd never been especially close to Mael, but he deserved as much happiness with Rosealise as their chieftain and Jenna had found together. Indeed, the tracker had suffered much, perhaps more than any of them, and had earned the lady's heart. Fargas mag Raith had been a swine, pissing on everything good and dear to Mael.

And yet why cannae I feel glad of it?

What remained unbearable to Broden was not knowing if Rosealise had first been *his* lover. He could close his eyes and summon the memory of the lass in his dreams. Every time

her pale hair swept across his chest, cool and
soft, it had been the same pale gold. She'd
smelled of some dark flower he could not
name, but he knew the scent. He'd held her
and kissed her, and the splendid taste of her
mouth roused such desire in him that his
entire body had shaken with it. Yet the finer
details of her—her features, the sound of her
voice, what she had said to him—remained
lost to him.

As Rosealise had become, now that she
had chosen Mael.

Needing to put more distance between
him and Dun Chaill, he headed for the
mound. He paused only when a kestrel dove
down into his path.

"Return to the keepe, Falconer."

"My birds need to hunt," Kiaran said and
came out from behind a broad birch and fell
into step beside him. "I need to stretch my
legs. I reckon you need a brother's ear."

Impatience added a sharp edge to his
simmering temper. "If I slice off one of yours,
'twill no' grow back."

"You ken my meaning." The falconer's
gaze shifted, and the kestrel about to alight on

his gauntlet smoothly soared back up into the canopy. He dropped his hand. "'Tis odd. You leave while Rosealise speaks, and yet hide to listen where she cannae see you. I cannae fathom your reasons."

Broden stopped and regarded him. "Do you become a female now, that you must trot after me and beg my confidence? Go prattle to Edane."

Kiaran patted his crotch. "No, still yet a man. You arenae Edane's favorite matter of late, and the chieftain worries on you." His expression grew sober. "'Tis the kind path I wish to take here, as a brother, to offer you consolation. Mayhap some counsel."

"I'm no' a wench, you're no' my kin, and Domnall needs tend to his own facking concerns." Broden jerked his head toward the keepe. "You've seen to your duty. Begone with you."

The falconer sighed. "The manly path, then."

Broden's head snapped back as Kiaran's fist plowed into his jaw. He snarled and lunged, knocking the other man to the ground. Kestrels shrieked overhead as he and the falconer tussled, fists and elbows and legs churning. Broden managed to clout him hard enough to make him wheeze before Kiaran drove his knee into his side, flipped over him, and scrambled to his feet. Broden did the same, a dull roaring filling his ears.

"Now, brother, recall that I'm rather fond of my face," the falconer warned as he circled, mirroring his moves. "It maynae be as pretty as yours, but 'tis precious to me."

In that moment he heard Rosealise's pretty voice in the kitchens again, and the words that had crushed his hope.

Any time we have left is precious to me.

Mael had become hers, and she his, and nothing remained for Broden but to accept.

The fack I shall.

He rushed at Kiaran, his fury erupting in a bellow of rage, only to be smacked in the face with claws and feathers and screeching.

The small bird pecked and clawed as if intent on removing Broden's face a pinch at a time. If it had been the falconer, he would have defended himself, but the delicate bones of the fierce kestrels could not withstand even the slightest blow. He halted and squeezed his eyes shut to protect them, staggering until he felt Kiaran come near.

"Enough, Dive." The falconer gently pried the furious little raptor away. "I'll fight the arse myself."

Trickles of blood ran down over Broden's lashes from the scratches on his brow, which Kiaran mopped away with his sleeve. When at last he looked into the falconer's midnight eyes, he saw the gleam of mirth.

"If you laugh at me now," Broden muttered, "I shall cut off your head. This night, while you sleep."

"Then my birds shall hunt you." The falconer released Dive, who flew up to join the four kestrels circling over them. "And the next time, my friend, they'll blind you first."

"Gruesome wee fackers," Broden muttered and spat a short feather from his mouth. "Why do you name yourself my friend?"

Kiaran shrugged. "We're much alike. Mag Raith by fate, no' by tribe. 'Tis an odd kinship, but one we alone share."

An uneasy shame filled Broden as he saw how indifferent he'd been to the falconer's unstinting camaraderie all these centuries.

Even after they'd awakened in the grove, he'd
paid no mind to how the other man might
have felt to be stranded with the other hunters.
Domnall, Mael and Edane had the bonds of
their shared blood line. Like Broden, Kiaran
had lost all his kin, but long before they had
set out on that final hunt.

He put his hands on the falconer's fore-
arms. "'Twas foul of me to spill my spleen on
you when you but wished to annoy me. Had
you a heart, I'd ask your forgiveness."

"Aye, and you're an arse with boils. I've no
notion why I bother with you." Kiaran
returned the clasp of comrades briefly.
"Come. I'd like another look at that hoard."

He accompanied Broden to the mound,
but said nothing more. The trapper was glad,
for melancholy had replaced his anger, and he
might say more than he wished to. When they
reached the hoard, they stood beside the smol-
dering remains of Edane's latest fire, in which
he had burned a heap of ruined wool. On the
other side of the widened opening the archer
had also begun sorting and stacking useable
goods.

"The tools shall be welcome," Broden

said, nodding toward the archer's neat pile of unearthed implements. Although many appeared rusted, and had rotted handles, the heavy forged metals looked sound. Working to improve them might keep him from brooding on Rosealise, too. "We've some ash I may carve and fit for new grips."

"We might reuse old iron as well by smelting and recasting it. To earn my keep with the tribe I worked their forge." Kiaran toed a scorched coin from the ash. "The chieftain maynae wish Roman goods in the keepe, but we may turn them into Mag Raith goods."

His invocation of their tribal name made Broden think of Eara. The Pritani lass who had loved him, and who his sire had scorned him for it before the entire tribe, sometimes still haunted him. The only person in his life to love him, she'd suffered much disgrace and humiliation for her affections. Once she had been married off to the tribe's smith, he had kept far away from her and her mate.

"How many bairns do you reckon Eara birthed?" Broden asked idly.

"None. Her mate couldnae sire any." Kiaran nodded at his surprised look. "A horse trampled him as a lad. A hoof to the baws gelded him. 'Twas why he grew so fat, you ken. He yet doted on her."

"Aye." In their mortal lives Domnall had sometimes spoke of the lass, who after her mating had lived very well in the finest of *brochs*. The taciturn smith had seen to her every comfort, even bringing in other lasses to see to the cooking and cleaning. "'Twas why I never stole her from him. I wished that life for her, that I couldnae give."

"You cannae give Rosealise any kind of life," Kiaran said as he picked up the coin, idly rubbing the soot from its face. "The white plague shall take her by winter."

"The Sluath struck down Jenna with lightning," Broden reminded him, "and Dun Chaill made her immortal."

"Did it, now." The falconer frowned as his gaze shifted in the direction of the keepe. "I wonder."

Chapter Seventeen

ADDING WOOD TO the fires in the great hall gave Rosealise something to do as she waited for Mael to return with the chieftain. The tonic Edane had prepared for her had proven quite unpalatable, but she could not deny its soothing effects. Even the smokiest of the hearths had not caused her to cough.

"Pinch your nose before you drink," the archer had advised her. "And chew some mint leaves after you've swallowed."

The mint had indeed helped.

She looked about the empty hall, ill at ease with nothing to do in the household. Everyone had hurried away, busy with their tasks. Idly she returned to the table, where the scroll map still lay. Unrolling it, she sat down to study it again. The blue ink used to draw it appeared very dark, and the parchment so flexible and sound as to be newly-made. It might have been done only yesterday, and yet Jenna had assured her no one had lived in Dun Chaill for centuries.

"Perhaps the magic of the arch kept it pristine," Rosealise murmured under her breath.

She traced a path on the map from her chamber to the great hall. Directly above her finger sat a rectangle in which had been drawn an arch filled with blank ovals in staggered rows. Judging by the position of the inset detail to the larger area of the map around it, it suggested the great hall contained another hidden archway.

Rosealise looked up and studied the walls around her. As in her chamber, they appeared to be solid stonework. She rose and went to the nearest to inspect it. Weather had scoured away much of the outer surfaces of the mortar, leaving dark gaps between the stones. Remnants of yellow and red paintings still covered parts of each wall. None of the primitive designs of flowers and vines formed an arch, nor did anything interrupt their design. Tapping on the walls would yield nothing useful, she suspected, unless her touch disrupted the magic used to conceal the archway.

As she reached up to fit her fingers into a gap, the stroke of an unseen hand glided along her inked thigh. The tingling awareness between them had a decidedly carnal feel to it now and she smiled.

"You are spying on me, sir."

"I didnae leave you here to climb the walls, lass," Mael said from behind her.

"As it happens, I'm searching them." She turned and took in his unhappy expression before she gestured at the table. "A detail on the scroll leads me to think another archway was hidden here, in the hall."

"And now you seek it alone?" His scowl deepened. "These traps can kill, my lady, and if we never found you, I'd go mad."

Such a prediction might have pleased her before they'd been caught in the vine trap. Now it only reminded her of how foolishly she'd behaved.

"I am now aware of the dangers of these arches, Seneschal," Rosealise said. "I had no intention of entering it alone. I must do my part before my time comes to help keep you and your clan safe."

"Dinnae speak so," Mael said gravely. He strode over to her, and took hold of her hands. "You're strong, and Edane's clever. You've survived the Sluath. Dun Chaill healed Jenna–"

She pressed her fingertips to his mouth to stop the desperate outpouring.

"She was injured. I am ill. We cannot depend on it. For my part I will not waste another moment worrying on my affliction. You and I have much more gratifying experiences to share." She smiled as she watched him kiss her palm. "After we find this arch, if you would care to help me do so."

Mael's sigh slipped through her fingers. "Show me what you saw on the scroll."

After studying the map and listening to her theory, her lover pointed to her chamber. "'Tis no inset here to show the arch we found."

"Yes, but that trap's entry had been bespelled." Rosealise stroked a knuckle across her lip. "I wonder if the arch hidden here may be concealed by other means. A section of wall built on a pivot, to open as a door would?"

Mael nodded, and eyed the lowest seam where the walls met the floor. "If 'twas regularly used, opening and closing it might leave scrape marks on the old slates we found under the doss."

He walked with her along the walls as they inspected the pitted surfaces of the flooring stones. A few times Mael halted and crouched to touch the slate briefly, then shook his head and continued on with her.

"What do you see that I cannot?" Rosealise asked him.

"Much. When I awoke after our escape my senses had vastly sharpened." He glanced at her. "Bid me number your lashes from across the keepe, and I'd give you the true count. Whisper to me beside the stream, and I'll hear you in the kitchens."

"Surely not perpetually," she said, feeling alarmed now. Such an ability would cause him excruciating discomfort.

He shook his head. "Only as I wish to.

Hold, lass." He caught her arm and drew her back from a slate fitted in one corner. "Curving grooves, just there."

Rosealise peered at the stone, which simply looked worn all over to her. Then she eyed the arrangement of stones on either side of the wall seam.

"A corner makes a terrible spot for a hidden door."

He scanned the walls. "'Tis no' a corner." Putting out his hand, he covered the seam, which seemed to jump out from the stonework. "'Tis chiseled and stained to appear as such."

As soon as he took his hand away the faux stone began to move, rearranging itself to one side. A panel of wood, painted to appear as a corner, swung out from a dark space. The sound of clanking and scraping metal assaulted them.

"No' these bastarts again." He seized her and dragged her back with him as a metal statue of a man appeared and took a step out of the chamber. "Keep well back from them, lass. I ken how to stop—"

He shoved her back and ducked to avoid the rusted blade the statue swung at his head.

Without thinking Rosealise grabbed the statue's arm. "We are not your enemy. Stop this at once."

Speaking to it as if it were alive seemed supremely ridiculous, but the iron warrior turned his head to stare blindly at her. He then lowered his arm and went motionless.

Another came out of the hidden room, an iron dagger raised above its head. Mael swiped at some moss covering its head, and it fell over onto its side with a tremendous crash.

From the sound of metal grating it seemed more would follow these two. "You and your cohorts must stop attacking us," Rosealise told the first warrior. "We will do no harm here."

All of the sounds coming from inside the secret room went silent.

"Gods blind me," Mael said as he stared inside the dark chamber. "They've all gone still again." He gazed at her. "Your power persuades them, but they arenae living."

"Let us debate that after we summon the others and reseal this trap," Rosealise suggested.

MAEL WATCHED as Broden carried another of the heaviest stream stones into the hall. The trapper had tucked the sizeable boulder under his arm, as if it weighed no more than a sack of grain, and used only one hand to place it atop the others they'd piled in front of the corner trap panel.

Edane, who also watched him, rolled his eyes at Mael.

"'Tis enough?" the trapper asked as he surveyed the massive stone barricade.

"We'll see to cutting some timbers for bolt bars in the morning," Kiaran put in. "I can hammer some brackets to hold them from the old blades that cannae be salvaged as weapons."

"That should keep it sealed for the night," the chieftain said. "My thanks, Brother."

"Mayhap you should instead dig out the whole of the mound on the morrow, Kiaran," Edane suggested, his tone sneering. "Take Broden. He shall need use but a finger for that."

The trapper turned toward him, his eyes glittering.

"I, too, wish to thank you, sir." Rosealise stepped between the two men and smiled brightly. "Your gift of strength is rather astounding. We could not have managed this so quickly without you."

The trapper's jaw clenched as he glanced past her at the archer. When he met the Englishwoman's gaze he nodded once, and then abruptly turned and strode out of the hall.

"Rumble averted," Jenna murmured. "Nicely done, Miss Dashlock."

"Broden deserved praise, not scorn," Rosealise replied and frowned for a moment at Edane before she met Mael's gaze. "I should go and tidy up. Please excuse me."

"Sounds like a plan." Jenna kissed her husband before she retreated as well, leaving the four men alone.

"'Twill grow beyond words, this discord," Mael said to Domnall, who nodded his agreement. "We soon need settle it, else tempers reach for blade or bow."

"If you speak of me and Broden, tracker,"

Edane said hotly, "do so to me, no' the chieftain. I'm a man, no' a sick wench to be cossetted."

"Aye." Domnall folded his arms, his disapproval plain. "Very soon, Seneschal."

"Keep prodding tempers, Archer," Kiaran said mildly, "and we'll be digging up another hole, sized for you." He watched Edane stride out of the hall before regarding Mael and Domnall. "Those two arrange themselves as a deadfall trap. 'Twill no' take but one more nudge to trigger it."

"But 'twasnae set by Broden," the chieftain said, his expression growing thoughtful. "I'll speak to Edane on the morrow, after he calms. Fair night, Brothers."

Banking the hearth fires and extinguishing the torches gave Mael a few more minutes to brood. Although Edane and Broden had never been close, they'd seldom clashed so frequently as they had of late. The taunts and threats the two men now traded seemed born of natural dislike, but he sensed more behind it. Any suggestion of weakness set off the archer, who then made Broden the target of his ire.

Rosealise's illness also seemed to be involved in aggravating Edane, but how?

As he made his way to his chamber Mael decided to let Domnall handle his battling brothers. The chieftain had always kept the peace among them, and he commanded their respect. Mael had other, far more pressing concerns with his lady.

Aye, and pleasures.

It had been so long Mael had almost forgotten the delight of having a lover. The few *dru-widesses* who had come to share his bed had never stirred his heart, nor had they remained with him until morning. His lady had given him such satisfaction his body roused just thinking about it. He couldn't wait to have Rosealise in his arms again, and the thought of being with her hurried him down the last passage.

His chamber, however, stood empty.

Mael spied the tunic and trousers his lover had been wearing, neatly folded atop his bed, beside the heavy tartan he had left there. Since she had no other garments, he hurried down the hall to the old pantry. There Rosealise knelt just inside the threshold, wearing a shift made from sacking she'd somehow cut and tied together. She held a torch over the piles of wool Edane had brought in from the mound.

"Lass?"

"Edane's remark to Jenna earlier about the cloth made me curious. I took some sacks to make this shift." She rose and passed the torch to him. "If we fashion some bone needles and spin thread, there is enough here to make several garments for all of us. I would very much like to teach Jenna to sew clothing, and with her make a proper wardrobe for the clan."

"You neednae do thus," he assured her.

"Oh, but it would be such a…" Her face fell as she stared down at the pile of cloths. "…pleasure." She looked up at him, her eyes wet with unshed tears. "I will not be here long enough to do so."

Though Mael's heart clenched in his chest, he forced his voice to be light.

"Dinnae think on such things." He encircled her waist with his arm. "'Tis better to live in this moment."

Rosealise regarded him. "I will not live past winter. I told Edane the few months I have left are enough, but they're not." A gleaming drop slipped down from her lashes. "There's so much more that I want, and I have no time for it."

Mael brushed the tear from her cheek. "You have me, my *jem*, and I shall fill every moment that we share with joy. Let me be your strength, lass."

She accompanied him back to his chamber, where she stood before the hearth and looked down into the flames.

"We should speak about what happened tonight in the hall." She looked over her shoulder at him. "How could I control those iron men as I did?"

"I cannae guess. 'Twould be wise to ken how much power you possess," Mael admitted, and then an idea occurred to him. "We might fathom something of it together." He took hold of her hand, and laced his fingers through hers. "Persuade me remember the underworld, and what the Sluath did to us."

Chapter Eighteen

AS NIGHT SPREAD over the highlands, Galan surveyed the clear sky and frowned. For the first time he understood Prince Iolar's frustration. Without a storm, he and the Sluath remained earthbound. Flying over the ridges would have permitted him to quickly spot tracks and signs of the Mag Raith, and possibly follow them to wherever they now hid. Without use of his new wings he'd again become a weak, worthless mortal.

Aye, mortal, but no' druid kind. The weight of his decision to turn away from his faith had never been more onerous, for one misstep now and all he'd suffered would be for nothing. *I must attain the secret of immortality, or this life 'twill be my last.*

Galan felt a sharp edge cut into his palm, and smelled his own blood. He looked down to see he clutched too tightly the shell pendant carved with his dead wife's likeness. It dragged him out of his worry, and returned clarity to his thoughts. He might yet be mortal, but he would never be weak. For his beloved Fiana, and an eternal life together, Galan would suffer anything.

"Odd that we found no trace of the rebels," Danar said as they made their way back to the cave. "Even on foot they should have left some sign of their passage."

"If you think to blame me again, as Seabhag did," Galan said sharply, "consider the nature of your gates. The prince said the gates kill mortals."

"Yet you claimed Pritani magic the cause." The big *deamhan* stopped and caught his arm. "Was that a lie, Aedth?"

"Drag any druid here and they shall tell you the same," he snapped. "'Tis the only like-lihood. You made the Mag Raith immortal.

Only they could use their tribal spells and survive the gate's magic."

Danar released him, but then turned around to look toward the west. "How long has it been since the Pritani dwelled in these lands?"

"The tribes have been gone for more than a thousand years." Galan made an impatient gesture. "Prince Iolar awaits."

"Stop flapping your lips." The big demon crouched down, pressing his claws against the soil. He closed his eyes, and the air around him shimmered with Sluath magic as he reached toward Galan. "Give me your hand."

"What?" He recoiled. "Why?"

"I need some of the power that Iolar gave you for a magic seeking spell." His wings flared out, displaying the dozens of blades strapped to them. "Now take hold of me, or I will tear off your head and use your neck as my goblet."

As soon as Danar's claws curled around his hand Galan felt his power draining. Since resisting it might prod the demon to attack him, he instead focused on the magic flooding into the air. Although druid and Sluath spells had proven completely different, he felt the same spread of sensing that came from a seeking incantation.

Whatever Danar wished to find, however, did not reveal itself.

The power flowed back into Galan a moment later, and with a vicious sound the Sluath shoved away his hand.

"Doesnae your spell work?" Galan asked, feeling safer in playing the fool mortal.

"There's nothing of it." Danar gazed around them, clearly frustrated. "Nor could there be. It's long dead."

Galan saw the worth of having aided the demon. "Then we must report to the prince that we were unsuccessful."

A strangeness came into the demon's polished bronze eyes as he regarded him. "Never flout your failure to Prince Iolar," Danar warned him. "He tore apart the last Sluath who did. With the mood he's in, he won't show such mercy to you."

Galan thought quickly. "You all need shelter until we may reopen the gate. I ken a village no' too far beyond the ridges. They've no defenders, only farmers and drovers. I'll propose to lead you and the others to it. You may enslave the mortals to serve our prince's desires."

"A clever distraction." His steel-colored hair glinted as he nodded. "What will you do about the gate?"

"Can you use your seeking spell to search for Pritani magic?"

Danar confirmed Galan's suspicion by nodding. "As it's being used."

"We shall work together then. Use it to find and capture the Mag Raith's shaman, Edane. 'Twillnae be difficult if we take him when he's alone, for he's the weakest." The archer had kept Galan from killing Jenna Cameron, so he'd particularly enjoy seeing him suffer. "Then bring him here and persuade him reopen it."

The Sluath eyed him. "Now you begin to think as we do."

Chapter Nineteen

THE GLOW OF firelight enveloped Rosealise as she knelt down with Mael on the fur he'd spread in front of his chamber hearth. She suspected he'd suggested this to make her feel less wretched, but she now worried about what using her power might do to him.

"This seems unwise," she told him. "By forcing you to remember I might cause you some harm."

"The past cannae injure me, for 'tis done and gone. I ken that I'm safe in your hands, lass." Mael met her gaze as he reached out to her. "Try, and we may learn something more about our time together in the underworld. To ken how the Sluath changed me could save you, lass."

"I cannot see how." Being so close made her want to touch him, which wasn't helping her resolve. "You must not hope for the impossible."

"We're impossible, my *jem*," he chided. "A grand lady from the future, and a lowly hunter from the past, meeting twice in two different times? Naught could be less likely."

"I am not grand, nor you lowly." Rosealise saw how determined he was, however, and her own curiosity got the better of her. "If I see you in any discomfort, I will stop, and that will be all we do. Do you agree?" When he nodded, she slipped her palms over his. "Mael, tell me what you remember about the underworld."

"The white chamber. You with me. The spring pool, where we first loved." His fingertips glided over her skin, caressing her now. "I'd never felt such pleasure. You gave yourself to me so sweetly."

His voice purred with a masculine satisfaction that made her own desires swell. It had been real, and they'd become lovers in that terrible place.

"I wish I could remember it," she said, just as she realized she might not have to. "How did I give of myself?"

Mael's hands glided up her arms, and he pressed her back against the furs. Braced over her, he nestled between her thighs.

"Ye ever bid me do as I wished with ye, all I wished."

His voice sounded different now, deeper and rougher, with a much thicker accent. It seemed to reach inside her and wrap around that part of herself now going slick and full. Sparking sensations raced along her inked thigh, and she rubbed it against his hip. When she stroked his tattooed arm, she felt the same bright power beneath her palm.

All thoughts of discovering more about the past fled from Rosealise's mind. She needed her lover, and he wanted her.

"If you wish to reacquaint me with your wishes," Rosealise whispered, lifting herself so she could rub her pulsing quim against the thick girth of his erection, "I am most desirous to know, sir."

Mael dragged up the hem of her shift, baring her body to the top of her breasts. "I looked upon ye," he muttered, his gaze taking in her heaving mounds as he brought one big hand up to caress them. "And touched these pretty chebs. Ye made sounds as I put my mouth to ye that came as music."

Rosealise heard herself whimper the moment he began kissing her breasts, his tongue laving her hard nipples. He suckled and nipped at her while his fingers moved down her belly and between her legs. The enveloping heat of him sank into her, spreading a deep flush from her brow to her toes. One sensual stroke of his hand parted her, and she could feel her wetness greet him with a gushing fervency.

"'Twas naught ye wouldnae give me." He found the pearl of flesh hidden by her folds and caressed it slowly. Then he shifted his hand to penetrate her with two thick fingers, and slowly pumped them in and out. "'Twas so good, my lady, I hardly let ye slumber."

"No part of me wants sleep when you touch me," Rosealise whispered and drew his head down to hers. "What more did you put inside me, my titan?"

Mael rose up, smiling fiercely before he gripped her thighs. Then he bent to kiss her belly, sliding back as his lips roamed lower. Rosealise pressed her hand over her mouth to stifle a cry as he buried his mouth against her sex, his tongue plunging into her heated quim.

To be kissed in such a wicked fashion should have made her swoon, but it was too delicious. Seeing his face nestled in her thighs, and the hungry sounds he made added to the luxurious decadence of the act. He used his mouth with such avid, shocking skill that Rosealise became immersed in bliss. It was when he suckled her pearl that she thought she might drown in ecstasy. Somehow her hands now clutched his thick hair, and her hips jerked as her back bowed. With all her senses a-jumble she burst from the depths of aching delight to find him over her and his shaft plowing into her.

"Ye're mine," Mael said against her mouth.

He took her with hard, deep thrusts, his

body claiming possession of hers with ruthless determination. She came a second time as he did, unable to resist the pleasure he reignited. That long, shuddering climax made him groan as if he also felt it. Then he came out of her, clamping his hand around his shaft as his cock jetted his seed. He came on her belly and breasts, working his hand up and down as he painted her with his cream.

Rosealise roused from the drenching rapture to admire the gleaming streaks on her pale skin. "I wear you again, sir. I like it very much, but why did you do that?"

"'Twas so we wouldnae start a bairn." He took his hand and rubbed his semen over her skin, his expression almost thoughtful. "I feared I might, we loved so oft."

So Mael had tried to avoid making her pregnant in that dreadful prison. She understood why. To bear a child while a Sluath prisoner would have been horrid, and no doubt have ended badly for her and the infant, but it also saddened her.

"We would have made a beautiful baby together."

Mael gathered her in his arms and carried her to his bed before he pulled on his trousers.

"I'll warm some washing water for you."

You, not ye.

He'd stopped remembering their time in the underworld, and when she saw how miserable he looked she was confused.

"I am grateful to you for protecting me, Mael. I daresay if not for you I'd never have survived the wretched place."

He froze, and peered at her as if she'd insulted him. "I do naught but use you, my lady."

Rosealise sat up. "I don't believe that. What we did here we both wanted. Why do you hold yourself in such low esteem? Surely you see who you are, not only to me, but to your clan. You're the very best of men."

"I'm a bastart," he said flatly.

Her lover left the chamber before she could say anything more. What had she said to make him so unhappy? She rose to put on her sacking shift, and wrapped Mael's tartan around her before she hurried out into the hall. There she nearly collided with Broden coming out of the tower arch.

"Did you see where Mael went?" she asked him.

"Out through the old pantry." He nodded toward the other end of the passage before he peered at her face. In a much angrier tone, he demanded, "What did the tracker to you?"

"Nothing at all. I caused the harm to him by persuading him to remember the underworld." She brushed past him, and then stopped to glance back. "Why would you suspect otherwise? Mael has always been kind and gentle to me."

"Fargas mag Raith wasnae." His gaze narrowed. "Mayhap Mael recalled 'twas another who claimed you in that place."

Completely confused, Rosealise faced him. "I don't understand."

"You shall when you remember." He took a step toward her, his handsome face losing its near-perpetual scowl. "Only ken that you're ever safe with me, my lady. I vow it."

Rosealise suddenly understood a great deal about Broden's odd behavior. He'd formed a romantic attachment to her. Alarming as that was, learning why would have to wait for another time.

"I thank you for your concern, sir, but I am with Mael."

Broden looked for a moment as if she'd struck him. Without another word he turned and retreated into his chamber.

Chapter Twenty

E DANE WAS IN no mood to listen to Kiaran reprove him for the clash with Broden, and decided to spend the night under the stars. From the mound he took a soft hide bundled with strong cord, and set about fashioning it into a large swag bed. Tossing it over his shoulder atop his tartan, he strode past the mound into a grove of silver birch. The trees grew close enough together to allow him to stretch and tie the swag bed enough to fit his lanky frame.

He considered building a small fire to warm himself, but the light might draw more unwanted attention. Tomorrow would come soon enough, and with it another tongue-lashing from the chieftain. Tonight, Edane just wanted to be left alone and brood.

Broden likely now sits warming himself by a fire, the preening cock.

Ignoring the chilly lash of the night wind, Edane pulled off his boots and clambered up onto the swag bed. Once he'd settled himself, he shook out his tartan to cover his body. The hide swung gently with his movements, making the birches creak. The thick plaid smelled of the herbs he'd ground for Rosealise's tonic. He'd have to make much more of it before the dark, cold season arrived.

Gods, we'll have to bury her in winter. The prospect made Edane feel sick, and he closed his eyes. *I'll dig the grave after summer, and hide it until her time comes.*

He hadn't slept through the night since Rosealise had come to Dun Chaill. At first, he blamed the mound, and the gruesome aspects of the hoard within, but he never dreamed of violence or death. Rarely did he dream anymore. He'd take to his bed, sleep for a few hours, and then wake with his heart pounding and sweat soaking the ticking beneath him. To keep from waking Kiaran he'd leave the granary and take refuge in the great hall. There he'd doze off near the hearth, only to jerk awake again.

No memory of what caused his slumbering agitation ever came to him, but sometimes he heard himself mutter as he woke. He didn't understand most of the words, so he kept it to himself. Whatever plagued him kept him weary and on edge, especially around Broden. Of late he couldn't stop himself from goading the trapper at every turn.

Rosealise's gentle reproof came back to him: *Broden deserved praise, not scorn.*

Edane hated the other man's gift of strength, but what stirred his temper most was Broden's indifference to it. If Edane had the ability to rebuild Dun Chaill single-handedly, he wouldn't waste it cleaning chimneys or setting snares. He'd have put it to use at every turn. The mound he might have emptied in a day. The forest itself he'd have smashed into kindling.

Broden deserved to have his arse handed to him, bloody and beaten.

Wood bruised his palm until Edane realized he was still clutching his bow. Drawing it out from under the tartan, he held it up and watched the faint moonlight run along the polished yew. He'd dried the wood for two years before carving, and used oil and pine pitch to seal the grain. After centuries of fashioning his weapons Edane knew himself to be the finest bow maker in Scotland, perhaps the world. He never missed a target, either, thanks to the gift that he'd awoken with in the ash grove.

Like his own uselessness, his gift had no value to the Mag Raith.

He could make a hundred bows, and thousands of arrows, and shoot anything that moved within his sight. Edane had longed to become a superb hunter, and he had, only to awake to immortality to discover he could no longer abide hunting. Like the other hunters he had no notion as to why, but to use his bow on any living thing had become completely revolting to him.

The other side of the hated coin was his lack of ability as a healer. Despite all the old shaman's training, Edane could do nothing to save Rosealise. He hadn't the magic nor the power to cure her affliction, and he never would. In a few months the white plague would drown the lady in her own blood.

What cruel jests the Gods enjoyed.

Just before Edane drifted off, he felt something like the touch of soft lips on his cheek, and heard a low trill of laughter. He fell asleep before he heard the words that came with them, words that he knew he'd repeat again when he awoke.

Don't take any wooden nickels, you goof.

Chapter Twenty-One

꧁꧂

AS SHE HURRIED down the passage Rosealise recalled that Fargas had been the name of Mael's father, the brute he'd claimed that he closely resembled. But why would Broden invoke it? Surely, he knew the seneschal to be nothing like his sire.

Inside the old pantry she saw the door to the garden had been left ajar, and went through it out into the night. The glyphs on her leg grew warm as she made her way through the herb beds, and began to pulse as she approached the first wall of juniper. There she saw Mael's silhouette against a dark blue glowing gap in the towering hedge.

"No, please," Rosealise said, and stumbled

toward him. Her leg burned as if she were being branded again. "You know you can't go in there."

The seneschal didn't answer her, and when she reached him, she saw the grim set of his features.

"Return to the keepe, my lady." His voice sounded so defeated it wrenched at her. "Dun Chaill shall have its due."

"So now you become a lunatic?" She planted her hands on his chest and pushed him as hard as she could. He barely moved, so she shoved him again. "I will not allow you to feed yourself to this monstrous maze." She seized his knotted hands. "Why are you doing this? Is it because I forced you to remember something more than our love-making? What was it?"

"Torment. Fury." His eyes grew unfocused. "Pain."

The rough manner in which the last word burst from him sent a pang of the same through her heart.

"The Sluath hurt you?"

"No." He gripped her hands tighter. "I brought it with me to the underworld."

Rosealise frowned. "Do you mean that you were injured before you were captured?"

He shook his head, and beads of sweat began pouring down the sides of his face. He pressed his mouth shut so tightly it became a hard slash of a line. Whatever admission he was fighting not to make obviously distressed him, and she took her hands away.

"I told you that I wouldn't hurt you. Clearly forcing you to recall something so terrible does."

"No, lass. 'Tis what I've never forgotten." Mael looked into her eyes, his own reflecting the glow from the maze with a gleaming shimmer now. "You dinnae ken me."

"I know that I want you alive." Rosealise offered her hand to him. "Please, Mael. I beg of you. Come away with me now."

He stared down at her hand for several long moments, and Rosealise realized she might have to compel him to save his life. But finally he blinked, his massive shoulders sagged, and he took her hand.

She led him back through the herbs and into the hidden patch of berries. There the overgrowth hid them from sight, and the scent of the ripe fruit sweetened the dark air. Rosealise knelt down in the cool springy leaves, and drew Mael down with her. She took her hand from him and made sure they weren't touching.

"It was something that I said in your chamber, wasn't it?"

For a long time Mael said nothing. But as the silence stretched on, Rosealise forced herself to wait. Though she ached to comfort him and soothe his evident pain, she wouldn't add to it—not again.

"You reckon me the best of men," he suddenly said. "But I'm no'. I carry in my veins the blood of the worst."

Rosealise felt a shadow of agony as his words tugged at her. In the past they had spoken of this. She felt sure of it.

"You refer to your father."

"My sire," he said quietly. "Aye."

In a flat, unemotional voice Mael told her how brutal Fargas mag Raith had been to his wife, subjecting her to such savage beatings that he'd come close to killing her dozens of times. As a boy Mael had also suffered the same, but once he grew to manhood his father began to fear him fighting back. Fargas then turned all of his wrath on the helpless mother and her children, taking daily delight in the violence he wreaked on them.

It appalled Rosealise to learn that Mael could do nothing to stop his father's viciousness. Since the tribe believed men had the right to do as they wished with their mates and children, no one could interfere. Regarded as his property, they couldn't even escape.

"I've in me more than the blood of Fargas," Mael finally said. "His anger, his selfish desires, his viciousness, all shaped me. You saw that in the vision, when I returned from the arena."

"You are nothing like Fargas," Rosealise protested. "The Sluath forced you to fight for your life. As for this man you call your sire, that seems all he was. He gave you and your sisters life, but nothing more. Was he ever truly a father to you? Did he provide you with guidance and strength? Did he protect and support you? Did he ever once show you affection?"

"Never." He ducked his head. "Yet I didnae show him the love and respect of a son."

"Because he never treated you as one." She so badly wanted to touch him that she had to clasp her hands together tightly to prevent it. "And this is why you think yourself the worst of men?"

"You dinnae ken how much I hated my sire." He touched her cheek. "When you spoke of having my bairn, I saw how I'd deceived you. No female in my tribe would choose me as mate. They feared me the same as Fargas."

"I'm glad you never married any of them. They were simpletons." She kissed his fingers. "Was there anyone in this tribe of yours with a jot of sense?"

Mael closed his eyes for a moment. "Rosealise, I'm no' the man you think me."

"I know that you're the man who protected me in the underworld." She slid her hands onto his stiff shoulders. "I'm a very good judge of character, you know. As a captive I trusted you with my body and my heart. I do the same now."

Gently, he tucked her face against his neck. "Then ever shall I be as you would have me."

Chapter Twenty-Two

❧❀❧

I N THE SHADOWS Cul skirted the archer's makeshift berth, keeping his movements silent to avoid awakening the Pritani shaman. With the demons in the ridges so close to Dun Chaill, and unable now to return to the underworld, he had a rare opportunity at hand, and he would not waste it dodging his unwelcome tenants.

This could be the night.

After waiting so long for the chance to repay the Sluath for the ruin they had made of him, Cul could hardly believe it had arrived.

He climbed the gap in the southern curtain wall to the perch that allowed him full view of his kingdom. Although the magic of the maze had been triggered again, he sensed nothing had been caught and killed by its hedges.

Perversely it pleased him. The intruders had proven cleverer than he'd imagined.

The largest of the hunters emerged from the gardens, the Englishwoman on his arm. A faint tendril of their scents came to him on the night wind, making it plain they were in no state to face the demons. He waited until they disappeared into the castle before he did the same.

I must be calm, and think through this.

He'd not spent centuries building the greatest trap in history to squander it on an impulse of the moment.

Descending into the lower levels, he limped down a seldom-used tunnel to his armory. Although the archer had found the old leavings pit in the forest, Cul had kept the most useful items concealed beneath Dun Chaill.

Inside the silent chamber his torchlight fell on shelves of druid crystals and stacked scrolls, which together contained enough power and magic to level the castle. From the Roman invaders he'd wrested many fine *gladii* swords with ornately-embellished hilts, *plumbata* darts with tips that could be dipped in poison, and slender *dolabra* axes with skull-piercing picks. One foreign assassin who had nearly survived his battle with Cul had contributed a curved-bladed sica dagger bespelled never to miss its mark.

His treasures and trophies provided many satisfying memories, but to use them he needed the Sluath to venture inside Dun Chaill. With the hunters and their women remaining inside the spell barrier that protected the ruins, they would not attract the attention of the demons. To attack his enemy out in the open would lead only to Cul's exposure and quick demise.

Perhaps he could use one of the intruders to shield him and distract the demons. Or maybe he'd use all of them, since one might not survive long enough. Or he could...

A small smile curved his mouth.

Yes, of course.

He selected a carved stone before leaving the armory, and went from there to the warriors he'd placed in a store room beneath the tower. Moving among the motionless iron-clads, Cul selected one and released it from sleep.

"Come with me," he told the soldier. "We have much work to do."

Chapter Twenty-Three

"IF I AM to sleep through the night, I will need more of Edane's tonic," Rosealise told Mael after they'd returned to his chamber. He moved to go with her, but she held up her hand and nodded toward the cold ashes in the fireplace. "A little warmth when I return would be greatly appreciated."

He caught her hand and brought it to his cheek. Then he wrapped his tartan around her shoulders. "I'll warm you myself when you return."

The passage outside was dim. Earlier her lover had extinguished most of the torches, so only a few lit the way. The silence of the castle seemed more pronounced with every step she took, and as always, she felt as if unseen eyes were watching her.

My imagination gets the better of me again.

Moving through the shadows made Rosealise wonder about the underworld, and what it had been like outside the sumptuous cell she had shared with Mael. For the first time the luxury they had been afforded puzzled her.

Why had the Sluath pampered the captives that they otherwise used so abominably? She knew from the vision that they'd forced Mael to fight other slaves in their arena. She'd been dressed as a strumpet and expected to cater to his desires. If they had not formed such a close, passionate attachment–

The sound of stone scraping stopped Rosealise in her tracks. She peered through the tower arch that led to the buttery, and saw the gleam of moss-covered metal moving. Drawing back out of sight, she went still and watched.

An iron warrior walked through the arch and stepped through a gap in the stone. It was headed outside.

Where has it come from?

Only this afternoon she'd seen the secret arch in the great hall still blocked with massive stones. She needed to let Mael know. But when she glanced over her shoulder toward Mael's chamber, and then back to the moving statue, it was gone.

Where is it going?

In another few moments, she wouldn't even be able to hear it. She gathered the tartan tightly about her and hurried after it. Since it had no power of speech, she couldn't persuade it to tell her where it meant to go, or what had brought it out of hiding. Once she knew its destination, she would rouse the entire keepe. Losing it now might mean they'd never learn its purpose.

Outside, she just glimpsed it disappearing among the trees and quickened her pace.

She followed the iron warrior through the forest, and watched it cross the stream and continue toward the ridges. At the edge of the water Rosealise hesitated, glancing back toward the castle. If Mael hadn't fallen asleep by now he would be worried, and probably looking for her.

A flicker of torchlight suddenly lashed the

night sky, and Rosealise saw the iron warrior
halt on the trail leading up into the ridges. It
shuffled back, concealing itself in some brush.
She couldn't take her eyes from the bright-
ening light, for around it there seemed an
unnatural glow of white streaked with gold.
The colors wrenched at her, for they seemed
terrifying. Then something she had forgotten
came back to her, and she knew what
they meant.

Sluath.

Rosealise was trapped. For her to run
would draw the demons' notice, and to return
to the castle would lead them directly to it.
She had to protect Mael and his clan, even if
it meant her own capture. Quickly she waded
across the stream and hurried to the brush
where she joined the iron warrior.

Putting her hand on its arm, she
murmured, "I mean you no harm. You must
defend me if they attack."

The moss-covered head turned to look at
her with blind eyes, and then it drew the short
sword it carried and held it ready.

"The little village 'tis mayhap a league
from Wachvale," a deep voice said as a tall

man mounted on a horse rode down the trail toward the stream. The torch he carried showed plainly his deeply-lined face, which looked pale and grim. Beneath the back of his cloak a large, oddly-shaped mound bulged. "We shall arrive in but an hour, Prince Iolar. By then the mortals shall be subdued."

"If my *deamhanan* met any resistance, Galan, I will have your head." Behind him rode a man of incredible beauty dressed in flowing garments of white and gold. His perfect face twisted in a scowl. "Danar, did you instruct Seabhag to keep the females under guard?"

"As you commanded, my prince." At the prince's side a much bulkier, dark man appeared, mounted on a towering black warhorse. Leather straps covered with knives and daggers crisscrossed his huge body. "None will be touched by our men until you've chosen those you want to attend to your pleasures."

Horror made Rosealise take in a too-quick breath. Her lungs constricted, and she clapped a hand over her mouth, but it was too late. The pressure in her chest was already building. The only way to escape would be if the Sluath would pass by before the coming coughing spate forced its way out.

The prince reined in his mount and sniffed the air.

"What is that?" he said, turning his face in her direction.

He swung down from his saddle and faced the brush where she and the iron warrior hid.

Blazes, he can smell me.

"Perhaps I will not have to wait after all." He breathed in deeply and smiled directly at the leaves and branches concealing Rosealise. "I detect a female alone, and ripe with such delectable fear."

The other men dismounted and flanked him.

"Show yourself," Galan ordered, his voice harsh. At the same time, he lifted his hands, which took on a faint glow. "Now, wench, or I shall use my magic to drag you out."

"Stand aside, you idiot," Iolar said as he came forward. He thrust his hand into the brush. "I'll not have you taint her with your spells before I sample her delights."

Rosealise clamped a hand around his

wrist, shuddering as soon as she felt the coldness of his flesh. "Forget me and leave."

"The little minx seeks to command me. How amusing." The prince groped for her, just missing her hand. "A shame she's one of your kind, druid. I might have saved her for when we return to—"

Iolar's fingers brushed against Mael's tartan, which he immediately grabbed. Instinctively Rosealise dug in her heels and yanked it back, just as the iron warrior struck the prince with his sword. The weapon slashed deep into the Sluath's forearm, and the demon howled and staggered back, falling against Danar.

The bigger Sluath grabbed the prince's bleeding arm and shouted, "Seize her, Druid, so I may cut her throat."

As Galan approached, he raised his glowing hands.

Would the iron warrior be able to protect her from the druid's power?

There was only a split second to decide, but she knew what she had to do. She screwed up her courage and lunged forward. Galan paused, his face clearly startled, as

Rosealise dove for his feet. She touched the druid's shin.

"No," she gasped. "Stop the Sluath from hurting me."

Galan froze. A huge bolt of power slammed into the Sluath behind him, who were blasted back against their mounts. They fell to the ground.

Rosealise clambered to her feet to survey the demons, who weren't moving. She couldn't tell if they were breathing, but their beauty seemed to be dimmed now.

Rosealise put her hand on Galan's arm. "Tell me, are they dead?"

"No. They're but stunned." As the druid stared down at her, his eyes focused and narrowed. "What do you to me?"

"Be still and let me think."

For a moment she considered telling Galan to kill them and himself with the warrior's iron sword. But from what they had said there were more demons waiting at the village. To do such a thing would lead them back here to take vengeance. In order to protect Mael and the clan she had to make this as if it had never happened.

"Put the Sluath on their horses and take them to the others," she told the druid. "Forget about me and what happened here. All you will remember about this night is that I attacked the demons, and you killed me for it."

Galan turned and went to the Sluath, grunting as he slung them over their saddles. He gathered the reins before he mounted his horse and led the other two down the trail. Once he reached the glen he turned away from the stream and rode away from Dun Chaill's protective forest.

The iron warrior shook beside Rosealise, and then fell over as a huge hand clamped over her mouth.

"Make no' a sound," Mael whispered against her ear, and tossed away the moss he'd removed from the warrior's head.

❧❦❧

MAEL WAITED until Galan and the demons had ridden out of sight before he released Rosealise.

She turned to face him. "However did you find me?"

"I'm a tracker."

He took her arm and marched her over to where he'd concealed his own mount. Without another word he tossed her up onto the horse's bare back and swung up behind her.

As he took her back to Dun Chaill Rosealise told him of following the iron warrior to find the druid and the two demons. Mael said nothing, and barely heard the words she spoke. Seeing her so close to Galan and the Sluath, to death itself, still enraged him.

When he reached the crumbling ruin of the curtain wall, he held her against him as he dismounted, setting her on her feet.

"You must be dreadfully annoyed with me," she said, and reached out to him. "It was foolish of me to follow–"

"Go inside, my lady," he told her through his clenched teeth. "I beg you."

Rosealise gave him an uncertain look before she nodded and retreated into the castle. Mael saw to the horse before he went after her. In the great hall he found her speaking earnestly to Domnall and Jenna.

"I didn't know what else to do," Rosealise was saying. "I thought if they saw me running back here, they would surely follow, and find you all."

"'Twas a wise if reckless choice. The Mag Raith owe you a debt." The chieftain met Mael's gaze. "Seneschal, what saw you?"

"Galan and two Sluath, allied against us. Doubtless sworn as brothers." The words came out of him snarled and bitter. "The druid has gone too far this night. He wishes to follow the dark path, aye, then I would chase him on it straight back to the facking underworld." He drew the axe from his shoulder harness. "I shall do so now."

"Alone? Dinnae be a fool." The chieftain turned to his wife. "Jenna, 'tis late, and I'd speak more on this with Mael. You and Rosealise should seek your beds."

"I beg to differ, sir," the Englishwoman said. "I witnessed all that occurred, and heard much more. I would be included in your discussion."

"Included?" Mael stared at her in disbelief. "'Tis only by the grace of the Gods you yet breathe, my lady. Do you ken what they'd have done to you? To my brothers and sister as they slept, unaware?" He threw out his arm. "Look upon this hall. Had those fackers found Dun Chaill, 'twould be painted red with our blood."

She paled as the shouted words echoed through the passages, and she turned away to cough against her sleeve.

Instantly chagrined, Mael reached out to her. "Rosealise."

"I did mean to come back and tell you of the iron warrior," she said, turning to face him. "I had no notion of what would occur in the ridges. There was no warning. When I saw the demons, it was already too late to flee." She regarded Domnall. "You must know that I would never have led them here. I'd rather die first than betray the Mag Raith."

Even now she had so little regard for her life.

"You should be dead," Mael told her flatly. "For that is what you chased into the ridges this night, my lady. Your death."

"Gently, Brother," the chieftain said, in the tone of a stern warning.

"Maybe this isn't the best time to talk," Jenna said, as she took hold of Domnall's hand and gave it a tug. "We're safe for tonight, my man. Let's do this in the morning."

"I think more needs to be said," Rosealise said. Her voice took on a strange tenor of calm. "It was wrong of me to leave the castle alone, and I apologize for putting you and your clan in danger. None of my actions were deliberate, however, and I will not have you speak to me as if they were otherwise."

"'Tis no matter if you willnae protect yourself. I shall." Mael strode up to her. "Never do you leave the castle again. If you wish something beyond these walls, bid me or one of the others fetch it. If you dinnae heed me I'll chain you."

"I see." Rosealise slowly removed his tartan and placed it over his shoulder without touching him. "I am not your captive, nor yours to command."

"I'd see you kept safe, my lady."

"You overstep my trust, sir." She turned away from him. "Chieftain, if I may borrow your wife, I would retrieve the bedding from my old chamber. I will be occupying the buttery now, if you deem it safe."

Domnall nodded, and the two women left the great hall.

Stunned now, Mael started after Rosealise, only to find the chieftain in his path.

"I'd explain to her my meaning," Mael said. "Step aside."

"You've said enough." Domnall jerked the axe from his grasp. "Jenna has driven me to such fury, so I shall give you pass. This once." He stepped in closer, his eyes glittering. "You take hold of yourself and your temper or I'll put *you* in chains."

The chieftain dropped the huge weapon at Mael's feet and stalked out.

Chapter Twenty-Four

S MALL MOTHS FLEW at the odorous tallow candles lighting the close confines of the hovel. They cast fleeting shadows across Galan's damp face. He'd been so intent on bringing the two unconscious Sluath to the village that his thoughts stretched beyond that goal only after arriving. Thinking of the ridges brought back only snatches of images and sound. Try as he might, he could recall almost nothing of the attack. But the jumble of his memory didn't worry him as much as the prospect of what would happen if Prince Iolar never again awoke.

My life and hopes, destroyed by a facking wench.

"Tell us again what happened," Clamhan said from behind his skull mask.

"We left the cave to start for the village. Our prince detected a mortal female in hiding. She attacked him and Danar, and I ended her for it," he said, sure of his claim if nothing else. "I put them on the mounts and rode here. 'Twas naught but that."

Across the crude table Seabhag thrummed his claws against the pitted wood. "You expect us to believe that a mortal bitch struck down the two fiercest, mightiest of *deamhanan*. Then you, a fucking tree-licker, killed this marvel of the ages."

"'Twas likely a powerful druidess," Galan replied. He met the demon's eyes, which remained black and gleaming in his constantly-shifting face. "Never did I see her. She took the prince and Danar by surprise. 'Twas but the Sluath power bestowed on me that stopped her."

"He lies," Meirneal said. "Again." He came around the table, his cherubic features glowing with glee. "Give him to me, Clamhan. I'll bite him until he confesses. I can make him last for a week, perhaps longer."

"Leave the druid alone," a weary voice said from the pallet by the hearth.

Galan looked over as Danar rose stiffly and came to join them. "I'm glad you survived the wench's magic."

"That was no wench," Galan said, probably for the tenth time.

Danar glanced around the hovel. "What have you done with the prince?"

"We put him in with the females still healthy enough to serve," Clamhan said and spat at Galan. "Your pet druid didn't mention this village is gripped by plague. Most of the mortals here lay dying of it. Their senses have grown too clouded by the sickness. They're little more than rotting, moaning meat."

"How could I ken thus?" Galan retorted. He regarded the big demon. "I've been among you since leaving my own tribe."

"Not every moment," Meirneal said, and bared his tiny teeth. They elongated into small, sharp fangs. "I starve for quivering flesh. Let me feast on him, Danar."

As the diminutive fiend lunged, Galan pushed back from the table. But he needn't have since Danar grabbed him by the curls and dragged him back.

"Control yourself, you little fool," he told Meirneal. The Sluath shrieked as Danar flung him to the ground. "Galan, with me. Clamhan, take us to Prince Iolar."

The masked demon led them from the hovel to a larger, finer cottage near the center of the village. There four Sluath stood guard, each in the guise of huge mortal mercenaries. Galan followed Danar inside to find the big front room crowded with cowering mortal females who had been bound together in a circle around a bed. The prince lay atop the fur-draped ticking, his wounded arm wrapped in black-stained bandages. The glow of his magnificent form and his godlike countenance appeared muted, as if slowly being snuffed out by some unseen force.

Danar stepped over two sobbing wenches to kneel beside the bed. "Has he stirred at all?"

"No," Clamhan said. He moved to the other side, but the sight of his skull mask made the female cry out in terror. *"Silence."*

"Druid, come here," Danar ordered, and

when Galan joined him, he gestured at the prince's ashen face. "Did Sluath magic do this?"

"The only demons there were you and our prince," he pointed out.

"The only *deamhanan* that you saw." The big demon gestured at the prince. "What does this to him?"

Galan put his hands above Iolar's face, but the moment his power touched the enchantment it ended. As the prince's eyelids stirred his glow intensified, restoring his beauty.

"'Tis as 'twas in the cave," Galan said. "Pritani magic. I've broken the spell." He wasn't sure how he'd done so, but had no hesitation over taking the credit for it. "The Mag Raith shaman, Edane, must have used a mortal female in the ridges to lure us close."

Danar looked skeptical now. "He struck the prince with an iron sword, which he knew could kill us both. Why would he resort to wielding magic when he had the advantage of the weapon?"

"Iron wouldnae slay me," Galan said quickly, "and Edane's a weakling who ever feared my magic." Had the shaman cast a spell to remove his memories, it would explain why he couldn't recall the events clearly. "When I ended the wench, doubtless he saw how 'twould turn for the worse for him, and fled."

"So it would seem," a weak voice said. Iolar slowly pushed himself up and surveyed the trembling, frightened females around him before he met Galan's gaze. "You served me well tonight, Druid. I will not forget it. Now get out."

Galan followed Danar out of the cottage, from which screams began even before the door slammed shut behind them.

Chapter Twenty-Five

MAEL'S ABSENCE FROM the morning meal and Rosealise's unhappy silence suggested to Broden that the two had quarreled. After the ladies left to attend to the kitchens, Domnall briefly recounted the events in the ridges during the night.

"Kiaran, you and Edane gather what iron swords and daggers you may find in the mound," the chieftain said. "Bring back all still fit for use, and what more we might employ as protection for the ladies. Broden, you stand sentry in the hall until our return. Jenna and I shall move the horses to shelter in the forest out of sight. Once 'tis done, we shall see to barricades."

"What of Mael?" Broden couldn't help asking.

"He patrols the edge of the woods by the stream to keep watch for the demons." Domnall's expression tightened. "'Tis likely Rosealise insured they willnae return by persuading Galan to think her dead. If no', we must stand ready to defend the castle."

"Mayhap we should consider fleeing to the west," Kiaran said. As the other men regarded him, he sighed. "I ken 'tis the coward's path, but we've females among us now. We must think to their safety. The Sluath cannae kill what they dinnae find."

"Wachvale willnae give us sanctuary," Domnall said. "Nor could they or any village withstand a demon attack. 'Tis two days' ride over open ground to the midlands." The chieftain shook his head. "I'll no' risk it. We're better protected here, behind what walls yet stand."

Broden saw something like pain flicker through the falconer's eyes. He knew Kiaran to be as brave as the other hunters, but this talk of fleeing came from more than fear of the Sluath.

He ran from the Vikings when they attacked and slaughtered his tribe, but he's no more a helpless lad.

Kiaran caught his look and grimaced before he regarded Domnall. "As you say, Chieftain."

After the other men left, Broden lit all of the torches and checked the surrounding passages while surveying what he could use against a demon siege. Lining the deeper holes in the ruins with swords and then covering them to appear as part of the dirt floors would serve as pit traps. With strategic placement of ropes and removal of mortar some of the crumbling stone walls could be pulled down atop an invading force.

When he returned to the hall Broden found himself looking down the passage leading to the kitchen. For a time, he was alone with the Englishwoman, and much could be said without worry of being over-heard, especially now with Mael far from the castle.

She doesnae want me.

After Rosealise had rejected him last night Broden had vowed to himself he would plague her no more. Yet countless other nights weighed on him now. He sighed and squeezed his eyes shut.

He'd dreamt of feeling his lover's soft hands stroking his body, and the low murmur of her longing against his lips. His skin yet warmed from the phantom feel of that long, moonlit hair sweeping over his flesh. The fragments of those hours together meant he had been loved by his lady, something he'd never known in the mortal realm.

If that had been his—if she had been his —he had to know.

Surely if Rosealise had given herself to him in the underworld she would not regret it. Jenna and Domnall proved that such love could be found again. He would ask nothing of her now unless she wished the same.

"Broden?"

He opened his eyes to see Rosealise standing only an arm's length away.

"My lady." By the Gods, but his own dreams had made a fool of him. "I should walk the passages."

"You've done that twice," she said, setting a basket of kindling wood by the hearth. "Come into the kitchens. I've just made a tea of sorts, and I'd appreciate a chance to talk with you."

Following Rosealise gave Broden nothing but more torment. She left in her wake the scent of herbs and berries, and the long spill of pale curls down her back seemed almost a taunt. By the time they entered the kitchens he could feel the sweat inching down his spine as he fought the grip of his obsession.

"Please, do sit down." She indicated one of the chairs Mael had made for her work table. From the hearth she took the brew pot and filled two cups. "This is a passably tolerant tisane of herbs, strawberry leaf and roses, with a touch of currant."

Broden hovered by the table, convinced he should be anywhere but there. Rosealise seemed as if nothing concerned her. She smiled at him as she brought the brew to the table and sat on one of the chairs.

"Rather hot yet," Rosealise warned after taking a cautious sip from her cup. "After last night I think we must dispense with veiled remarks and mysterious allusions. I prefer honesty over that. Do you agree?"

"Aye." At least his torment would end. "You should have your say first, my lady."

She inclined her head. "I'm aware that you've been watching me in a surreptitious manner every time I'm near you. From your expression I first presumed I caused you discomfort by my presence. Last night you made remarks that lead me to believe otherwise. When Jenna and I moved my bedding to the buttery, I concluded that we must discuss this unspoken matter."

He gingerly lowered himself into the remaining chair. "I thought you shared Mael's chamber."

"Not at present." She took from her pocket one of his snare cords and placed it on the table between them. "Yours, I believe. I found it in my bed."

Broden didn't touch it. "Likely dropped when I brought wood."

Her brows arched. "There was no need for a fire in there after I joined Mael. Nor could you have dropped it *under* my blanket, which was rumpled, as if someone had been sleeping there. No, don't walk away," she said as he got to his feet. "You agreed to speak plainly. Tell me what you were doing in my room. Why did you climb into my bed?"

Her directness freed him of all restraint.

"I put my face to your pillow, and wrapped myself in the blankets." Broden sat back down. "'Twas to smell your scent, and ken if 'tis the same as the lover in my dreams, the lady I left behind in the underworld."

She blinked. "Do you mean to say that I am she?"

"I cannae tell you. Her hair, 'tis the same pale gold as yours. Your scent isnae the same, but perhaps 'twas altered by distant memory." Before she could wheedle more details from him, he reached for her hand. "Do you dream of me?" He drew her to her feet, tugging her closer. "Do you wake wanting me there, my arms around you, my mouth on you?"

Rosealise placed one hand on his chest, but she didn't push him away for his boldness. "Never once, I'm afraid. You've mistaken me for another lady, sir."

"'Tis one thing I've never forgotten." He brought his fingers to her lips. "How 'twas to kiss her. The taste of her mouth. The feel of her against me. 'Tis driving me mad no' to ken if 'twas you, Rosealise."

A flush of color brightened her cheeks, but then she stunned him by moving closer. "Then you should kiss me now, and you will know."

While serving as defender to the Moss Dapple, Broden had taken many *dru-widesses*, but never had he kissed any woman but in his dreams. He put one arm around her waist, pressing her long body to his before he put his mouth on hers.

Rosealise allowed him to kiss her as he wanted without resisting. Yet it soon became clear to him that she took no more pleasure in it than he did. When at last he lifted his head, she looked into his eyes with nothing but compassion in hers.

Broden had his answer.

"You're ever kind to a bastart like me." He touched her cheek with the back of his fingers before he stepped back. "My thanks, my lady."

A guttural sound drew his gaze to the passage entry, where Mael stood with his axe in hand.

Chapter Twenty-Six

※❖※

I OLAR WALKED OUT of the cottage late in the morning to survey the mortal village. The stink of sickness blended with the fragrant flowers blooming across the pastures and small gardens. From the windows of the cottage the scent of blood added a coppery note. He had enjoyed the mortal females, whose simple minds had contained a sumptuous wealth of superstition and myth.

Their souls, however, had escaped him the moment he'd terrified the life out of their bodies. In the end it had all been a waste of his time.

Thin wisps of smoke rose from scattered, human-shaped piles of ash and charred bone. Their mounts had been penned with the villager's heavier plow and cart horses outside a small grain barn. Many of his *deamhanan* stood sentry on the roofs, watching the narrow lanes leading to and from the settlement. More had climbed the slopes, from which they scanned the skies for signs of favorable weather. All had glamoured themselves to appear as villagers. Upon seeing him each bowed before returning to their watch.

Iolar kicked the dirt under his boots. The place appeared little better than a cesspit, but until a gate could be opened it would have to do.

"My prince," Danar said as he approached with two guards, stopping a safe distance to bow. He looked tired and dim, but his gaze remained steady as he straightened. "We've taken control of the settlement and the surrounding land. Patrols guard the boundaries for two leagues. My scouts report that clouds approach from the west, and should arrive before dusk."

"Set fire to that hovel," Iolar told him, flicking his claws behind him. "Nothing in it still quivers."

Danar nodded to his guards, who trotted off. "How fares your wound?"

"How do you think? It fucking hurts." He looked down as Danar carefully removed the bandage to reveal the gash. As immortals the Sluath lived impervious to disease, but minor injury by iron required cautery. "Why didn't you sear it properly last night?"

"You recall your mood upon reviving, my prince?" the big demon countered. "I wished to leave you to your pleasures. I also prefer my head atop my shoulders, not stuffed up my ass."

"You're a wise coward. Very well, do it when I am distracted." Iolar sniffed the air and scowled. "Why do I still smell living mortals? Or is that my fault, too?"

"The druid suggested we keep the healthiest of the plague-stricken alive for other purposes." The big *deamhan* nodded toward a barn. "He has kept watch over them all night."

For a moment Iolar wondered if Galan had deceived Danar in order to save the mortals, and then discarded the idea. The druid had grown indifferent to the suffering of human kind, or he wouldn't have been able to tolerate the grafting of his wings.

"Remind me why I would wish to keep a great heap of whimpering, dying dirt-plodders on hand?" Iolar asked.

"I can think of no purpose, other than brief amusement," Danar admitted as he accompanied him into the barn. "But the druid swore you would approve. After he proved his loyalty to us last night, I was inclined to grant his request."

"Or you hoped it would enrage me enough to kill him. Don't worry. I'd have done the same." He rubbed his sore arm. "Take me to that idiot."

Inside the shadow-filled barn the low, dull moaning of the sick blended with the stink of their weeping sores. Galan had strewn hay under the bodies and covered them with blankets. Braziers glowed orange in the darkness as mounds of dampened herbs slowly smoldered upon their fat embers. Cries and groans rose in procession as Iolar trod over the mortals to where Galan crouched over a boy.

"I can't believe I have to say this to you, but Sluath do not coddle humans." He frowned as the druid drew the blanket over the young male's still, pox-riddled face. "Nor do we mourn their deaths. What the hell are you doing?"

"I'm keeping as many alive as may yet be usable." Galan rose and faced him. "Sluath have the power to restore them to health."

"In the underworld, yes. Here I can only revive them for a short time before they succumb to the plague. So, you wish me to save the mortals." Iolar looked up at the cobwebbed roof beams. "Have I taught him nothing, Danar?"

"You've instructed him at length, my prince." His second drew a dagger and used it to flick away the herbs from a brazier before he thrust the blade in the glowing coals. "The druid does not seem to learn."

"If you revive them as you say," Galan said, "I shall make them your creatures. Under my sway they will do whatever I command."

Danar chuckled. "Then they'll be *your* slaves, Druid. You ask for a personal army of the dying?"

"I wish to make them scouts." The druid told them of the dark magic he knew that would enslave the minds and wills of the plague victims. "Once they are bespelled I shall send them out to search for the Mag Raith shaman who attacked us in the ridges. He cannot be far from the spot, and he wouldnae suspect any mortal in passing."

"And when they find him?" Iolar demanded.

"They beg the Pritani to come to their village, to aid a dying druid they found in the ridges." Galan smiled. "While here we await his arrival."

Danar took hold of Iolar's arm, and before the prince could jerk it away, he applied the heated dagger to the gash. The searing pain made him hiss, but as soon as the *deamhan* took away the blade the gash slowly shrank and disappeared.

Galan stared, fascinated. "Fire heals you."

Iolar yanked his arm from his second's grasp. "Would you like to discover what it does to you, Druid?" Without waiting for an answer, he reached down to press his hand on the chest of a dying mortal man. "Drag the others closer, and we'll begin making your rotting scouts."

Chapter Twenty-Seven

ONE GLANCE AT Mael's face told Rosealise he had witnessed the kiss. His expression could be no more stunned than if the world had fallen down around him. She also suspected a lover's fury would follow his shock, and would be taken out on Broden.

That she could not allow. "My dear sir—"

"Take your hands from her," he said through his teeth, his eyes so dark now they looked black.

Broden stepped away from Rosealise, but the guilt in his expression perplexed her.

"'Tis no' what you reckon, Brother. We but spoke—"

"Alone here, and my bed still warm from

her." The big man took a step toward him. "Oh, aye, I ken what you do, you conniving bastart."

"You are quite wrong, sir." Knowing no other recourse, she put her hand on the trapper's arm. "Please explain precisely why you kissed me just now."

"I wished but to taste her lips," Broden said, his tone almost apologetic. "'Twas to test my remembrance of a lady I kissed and loved in the underworld."

"Loved?" Mael spat out the word. "To do thus, when you ken of my regard for Rosealise. How couldnae you look upon her and ken?"

"I cannae recall the lady's face, only the shade of her hair," the trapper countered. "'Twas the same as Rosealise's. She granted me the kiss, but felt no desire, nor I for her. She's no' the lady of my dreams."

She took her hand from Broden. "Mael, that is the truth. Broden and I remain friends, but that is all there is, or ever will be, between us."

Her lover's head lowered, and his shoulders shook. Suddenly he roared and hefted his axe, and slammed it into the work table, cleaving it in two. As the wood split and their brew cups fell and smashed, Broden drew his sword and shoved her behind him.

"Rosealise, go to the forest and find Domnall," he said quickly. "Stay with Jenna, and bid him return at once."

"You chary fack." The big man tossed his axe down to clatter on the slate floor. "Ever still you regard me as Fargas, when I've never once given you cause. You ken I'd hack off my very arm before I'd smite any female, or a man I considered my brother. Never again, Broden."

"As you say." The trapper's eyes narrowed, and he jerked his chin at Mael. "Yet you crept in here to spy on the lady. She gives you her affections and you treat her as property, no' beloved. Leave Rosealise in peace, and I shall believe you."

"Aye, but I've more to say, to her." Mael regarded Rosealise. "I nearly lost you last night, so close to death you came. The harsh words I spoke, the threat I made, all came from the grip that terror had upon me. Fear begets anger in me."

"Then you will always be angry with me, for I draw closer to death every day." She went to him, and caught his hand in hers. "You cannot keep me sequestered in the castle and wish it to revive me after death as it did Jenna. I know that hope spurred you to speak as you did last night, not my foolishness. Mael, you must accept my fate."

"Ken that my heart, 'tis yours, my *jem*." He touched his brow to hers. "But for as long as you draw breath, I shallnae accept your fate."

Rosealise blinked back the sting of tears. "That I cannot accept, sir."

"Then you ken my quandary. I must patrol now." He moved back and took a bundle from his belt. "More herbs for the lady's tonic, as this dawn Edane bade me gather." He tossed it to Broden, who caught it with his free hand. "The true reason for my return to the castle."

Mael scooped up his axe and left, and Broden released a heartfelt sigh. When he turned to her Rosealise saw his handsome face had grown pale and damp. The hand in which he held his sword also trembled slightly.

She had caused this unhappy situation, which lately seemed to be all she did. At least she could reassure the trapper that he had not been the cause.

"What Mael said to you... You must see that he's very angry," she assured him. "Once he's had time to calm himself and think it through, I'm certain that he'll regret it."

"I earned every bit of it." He sheathed his sword. "'Tis all truth. Naught fills my heart but hatred. I've no' cared for another but myself. 'Tis ever been thus."

"Codswallop," Rosealise said firmly. "You spoke with great affection of the lady you met in the underworld. I suspect you concealed your dilemma regarding me out of your regard for my lover. Jenna told me that you've done nothing to Edane to earn his contempt."

"I've taunted him too many times," Broden said, sounding weary. "'Twas my sire's way with me, and I reckoned would toughen his sensitive hide. Edane would laugh to ken that in our mortal lives I ever envied him. As a lad he didnae thrive, and still his kin doted on him. His sire sought for him every comfort and ease."

"While you had little or none, and had to be strong to endure," she guessed. A sudden thought made her peer at him. "You could have easily used your great strength against Mael, but you instead drew your sword. Why?"

""Twas at hand." He sounded uneasy now. "Mayhap the next time we quarrel I shall clout him."

"I think you'd sooner take up chimney sweeping." Rosealise was finally beginning to understand the trapper's surly nature. "You never defend yourself with your power, do you? You know what it can do, but you don't wish to hurt the other men. Just now you were afraid not of Mael, but *for* him."

"I'm but a man, my lady," Broden said softly. "And I've a temper, just as Domnall and Mael and the rest. Only I may never truly unleash mine. My brothers oft forget this, but I cannae." He glanced down at his hands. "I dare no'."

"You serve as a fine example to me." An incredible gift that doubly served as a perpetual burden, and yet Broden bore it without complaint. She would learn to do the same with her own. "I believe that proves beyond everything that you have a good, kind heart, my dear sir."

His gaze grew remote. "You but ken me in this life, my lady."

Edane came in from the gardens carrying a heavy mound of sacking-wrapped blades.

"Kiaran follows with iron shields on the sled. He reckons we may use them to…"

His voice trailed off as he looked from the ruined table and shattered crockery to the trapper.

"Say naught to me," Broden warned him.

He shoved the bundle of herbs atop the swords before striding out. The archer's jaw sagged as he watched the trapper go, and then he eyed Rosealise.

"Do I now slight him by breathing?"

"No, but he's had a trying morning." She took the herbs to set them aside, and then noticed the color of the blades he'd brought. "These swords are made of iron?"

"Aye. 'Tis the only metal that may slay the Sluath." He put down the bundle. "What of it?"

Rosealise thought of the iron warrior left

behind in the ridges, and the sword he had carried, and then looked around the kitchens.

"Everything made of metal that I've seen inside the stronghold resembles iron, but it's not. I believe it's all made of bronze."

Edane looked perplexed. "How could you ken thus?"

"By my cleaning, sir. Iron takes on a reddish-orange patina when it rusts, as you see," she said, gesturing to the swords. She then took the cooking pot from the hearth's edge and showed him the corroded patches she had not scrubbed from its outside. "Bronze turns black, brown or green."

"'From the copper and tin used to make it, aye," the archer said thoughtfully. "The first Pritani forged in bronze, but 'twas long before the Mag Raith. Iron 'tis harder and stronger."

"Yet the builders used bronze inside Dun Chaill." Rosealise set down the pot. "Only the warriors are made of iron."

Edane's brows rose. "Mayhap we're no' the first to battle the demons."

Chapter Twenty-Eight

MAEL PATROLLED THE edge of the forest until dark, when a wide bank of storm clouds blotted out the last of the sunset. He walked down to the stream to watch the approaching storm with his far-reaching sight. None of the tell-tale flashes of light that heralded the Sluath riding the clouds appeared.

"Any sign?" Domnall asked as he joined him on the bank.

"Naught on the ridges or above them." He waited for the chieftain to pour his scorn on him for the clash in the kitchens, but the other man remained silent. "You should ken that I near brawled with Broden this morn."

Domnall eyed him. "If I'd found him with

hands and mouth on my lady, I'd hurl more than harsh words."

Doubtless Rosealise had related the confrontation to Jenna, who kept nothing from her husband. The chieftain's understanding, however, eased some of the weight on his mind.

"The trapper yearns for a dream. I ken the sting of finding such, only to have it snatched from my grasp." He'd offered the lady his heart, and she'd refused it, but that was her right. "She'll no' forgive me, will she?"

"I'd spare you the answer to that, Brother, but we need you in the stronghold this night." The chieftain frowned up at the heavy clouds. "More than the prospect of the Sluath returning sets my teeth to grate. The appearance of the scroll map I only doubted, but the iron warrior luring Rosealise from the keepe direct to the demons, 'twas no' by chance."

Mael nodded. "Something beholds us that we cannae see, and puts us to dark purpose."

"I dinnae believe in *kithan* or spirits," Domnall said, "but this watcher may employ magic to conceal its presence at Dun Chaill. 'Twould explain much we couldnae fathom."

"A *dru-wid*, then, one following the dark path, like Galan." He nodded toward the ridges. "One who carries a grudge against the demons."

"Or fears them," the chieftain countered. "'Twould be reason to fashion iron warriors to defend the castle. Aye, and the bespelled traps. Come."

As they walked back through the forest to the stronghold Mael considered how they might discover the hidden foe.

"If we openly hunt the watcher, he'll ken," the tracker said. "We must use cunning, as with a wounded animal."

"The falconer and his kestrels can patrol from the air," Domnall said as they walked back through the forest. "Yet we need measures put inside the stronghold. You must become our watcher now. Edane may best ken how to reveal this bastart."

Domnall said nothing about Broden, but Mael guessed he'd put him to a similar task as well.

"Should we find this watcher, what then?"

Domnall stopped at the edge of the trees and looked for a long moment at the ruins.

"We gave twelve centuries of service to Galan and the Moss Dapple. Before that, our work went to our kin, and the tribe. No more do we serve the wonts of others. We're a clan now, and 'tis our stronghold. We fight for what's ours."

His calm assurance inspired the same in Mael. "Aye, Chieftain."

Inside the great hall Jenna sat finishing her evening meal with Edane, and looked up to smile at them.

"You two must be hungry."

"I must first speak with Kiaran," Domnall said, and after kissing his wife's brow left them.

Mael had no appetite, but to please the lady he sat down with them and shared their food. The flavorful fish pottage contained veg and herbs, attesting to Rosealise's deft hand, as did the seed-studded baked round Jenna handed him.

"In America we call this sourdough," the chieftain's wife told him. "Rosealise made the starter out of thin air, literally. I never imagined leaving a jar with wet oat flour outside in the garden would produce bread yeast, but your lady proved me wrong. Makes it worth grinding the oats by hand, which takes almost forever with a quern."

Mael knew that Jenna meant to put him at ease, but the praise for his lady made him wish the last twoday had never happened.

"Rosealise, she's well?"

The archer nodded. "Well and sharp-eyed. She found that the builders used iron to fashion the warriors, and yet bronze for all else in the keepe. I reckon they too fought the Sluath."

"The Bronze Age ended long before the Mag Raith came to the original fortress," Jenna chided. "It's more likely that they used up the iron available here while making the statues. Bronze became the only alternative."

Another time Mael might have joined in their talk, but he needed to see his lady.

"Where went Rosealise, Jenna?"

"She took some clean blankets to the buttery," she said, and grimaced. "She mentioned that it gets a little cold in there at night."

He thanked her and took his crockery to the kitchens before continuing through the new pantry to the darkened buttery. On its threshold he paused and looked in, and used his enhanced sight to inspect it. The ladies had arranged it into quarters, but only the blankets left atop the bedding attested to Rosealise's presence.

Mael glanced down, and spied boot tracks in the dust crossing the floor. Too small to be anyone but hers, they led out into the old pantry. He had no desire to hound Rosealise, but he could offer his help if she needed something more brought in.

He followed the tracks into the old pantry, but they didn't stop there. He saw how she had pushed aside a mound of wool to make her way into the far passage.

Mayhap she awaits me in my chamber. Mael recalled the gleam of tears in her eyes after he'd spoken his heart. *Or no'.*

He went to his chamber and saw Rosealise's tracks leading past it into the base of the tower. For the first time he saw other, larger tracks crossing hers. Whoever had left them had been dragging something to leave the long, scraping marks that distorted the footprints.

Rosealise had followed someone into the

tower, but had not come out. Mael approached the arch, but saw no one inside.

"My lady?"

No answer came. He moved inside, where he spied the map scroll on the stones, half-covered by his tartan. When he picked up the plaid it revealed a hatch that had been left open. A waft of cold air came up in his face, but it smelled of Rosealise, not dank and forgotten space. From deeper inside came the glow of a torch held out of sight. The remnant light it shed revealed a large, sunken chamber with two walls and a rope ladder hanging down from the edge.

Mael cast aside the tartan and map before he jumped down into the passage.

ॐ

WHAT ROSEALISE HAD THOUGHT to be a cellar stretched out into a seemingly endless tunnel. The torch she had brought lit the stone walls, but revealed no entries to other chambers or passages. Judging by its orientation, the tunnel ran beneath the old pantry back toward the buttery and kitchens. Here the stonework and mortar held firm, and no moss sprang from their seams.

"Mael?"

She turned around, even more perplexed to find herself alone. She had just seen him limping into the tower from his chamber, and had hurried after him to ask what had happened. Seeing the scroll and his tartan beside the open hatch had prompted her to follow him down into the cellar.

But it wasn't a cellar at all. A patch of wall with much finer masonry contained a large half-oval of grooves. Recalling the faux corner stonework in the great hall, she reached out to touch it.

"No," bellowed a deep voice.

A huge hand grabbed her wrist, making her jerk away.

"Unhand me, you– " She saw his face. *"Mael."* To see him appear beside her made her gulp in smoke from the torch and cough. When at last she recovered she gasped out, "Egad, sir, you startled the wits from me. What are you doing down here?"

"I came looking for you, lass, and tracked

you here. I saw the glow of your torch from above."

"That's unlikely, as I saw you limping down the passage ahead of me." She glanced down at his legs, which appeared uninjured. "Or perhaps Domnall or one of the others is having a joke on us."

Mael peered past her. "My brothers wouldnae do such. This man you followed, did you hear the sound of metal scraping as he limped?"

"No. I don't believe it was another iron warrior. He didn't move so stiffly as they do." She glanced around them. "This may be where the first was hiding, however. There could be more of them on either end of this tunnel."

He breathed in deeply. "I cannae smell iron, or anyone here but you." He turned his attention to her face, holding the torch. "Do you feel addled?"

"No, but I'm aghast at how easily I'm deceived." Her expression grew rueful. "I should have called out your name. I did not wish to press you to attend me if you did not wish—"

Mael jerked her into his arms and kissed her, lifting her up until her boots dangled. By the time he lifted his mouth from hers Rosealise had draped his neck with her arms.

"So, you still do want me," she said, her damp lips curving.

"More than breath." He set her on her feet. "Only we must climb out and fetch the others, and weapons. 'Tis how the bastart moves in and out of the keepe without our notice. He uses tunnels."

Before she could ask him to explain Rosealise coughed again, and turned away as the spate continued. Something burned her arm as her skin touched the wall, and she felt herself being pulled in to it.

"Mael."

He grabbed hold of her arm and tried to tug her from the now-glowing stonework. When it would not release her, he turned to put himself between her and the half-oval. But in response it yawned around him, sucking them both inside.

Chapter Twenty-Nine

CUL SILENTLY DROPPED from the half-fallen timbers he'd secured to hold his bulk aloft, and checked both passages flanking the tower before climbing down and closing the hatch. The torch the female had carried now lay on the stones, its flames slowly diminishing. He lifted it to inspect the masonry, which had solidified as soon as the gate had closed. The smell of her and the hunter still hung in the empty air. He reached through their scents to caress the finely-dressed stones.

"Rosealise." Her name rolled stiffly from his tongue, so he tried the other's. "Mael."

He had been right not to call to either of them. He could ape their movements, but the moment he spoke, his voice would have betrayed him.

Cul's plan had been to seal the gate once the female had gone inside, for he knew exactly what awaited her. Inflicting on her such an unkindness had seemed cruel, even for him, but her ability to control his iron warriors made her too dangerous. As a mortal she could be enslaved by the Sluath, who would use her as a weapon against him.

Iolar's little fiend had marked her, and would know of her power the moment he touched her. No, the female had to die.

Draping himself in her lover's tartan and luring her to the hatch had been a necessary risk. The ruse had worked just as he'd planned. Once inside the tunnel Cul knew that she would be drawn to the gate, as all who were marked by the Sluath would be. What he hadn't considered was that the hunter would pursue her. Now it seemed they both had fallen through together, and that would save the female. In a short time, they would remember everything taken from them, but they would never find their way back to Dun Chaill.

Or perhaps they will. They already escaped once...

Splaying his twisted fingers on the stone, Cul allowed himself a moment to wallow in the temptation. All that he had ever desired lay on the other side of the gate. He could kill the hunter, and take the female for himself. For a time, he'd know the pleasure that had been torn from him along with his life. But in doing so he would either kill her, or she would take her own life, and he would be alone again, and forever exiled from Dun Chaill.

Without his castle Cul was less than nothing.

"You are all I have, my beauty." He pressed his misshapen face against the wall, and let the cold stone scour his flesh. "I will never leave you."

Chapter Thirty

✦

AS THEY FELL into the yawning darkness behind the wall, the shroud concealing Rosealise's memories tore apart, bringing her back to the last day she'd spent in her time. As a governess in the eighteenth century, her life had been quiet, and ordinary, at least until she'd gone to Scotland.

Scotland...

The morning after the funeral, no maid came to dress Rosealise or arrange her hair. No tray from the kitchens arrived, either, although her chamber door had finally been left unlocked. It seemed the note she'd penned last night had reached the duchess after all.

The rest she would say to Her Grace's person.

Donning her best black gown, Rosealise flattened her unruly curls with a liberal application of mint-scented pomatum. Once she had inexpertly braided her thick mane she could manage only to coil and pin the long, lumpy cables, but her bonnet would cover the inadequate coiffure. Rosealise did not once consult the small looking glass. The Duchess of Gowdon didn't care how she appeared, nor did she give a jot for Her Grace's good opinion.

Blazes upon blazes, but she would be relieved to be done with that awful woman and quit this wretched place.

Rosealise left her room and carried her valise downstairs. Along the way, footmen, who should have offered help, pretended not to see her pass them. A maid carrying fresh linens gave her a wide berth, contempt shining in her eyes. Since young Lady Mary had died, Miss Dashlock no longer existed in their eyes. She knew this because they dared not fault the person truly responsible. The governess instead would forever be blamed for failing to save the child.

Would they be mollified to know what more Rosealise would suffer? Likely not. Servants could be greater snobs than the gentry, and they'd believe she'd justly earned her fate.

Rosealise put down her case to scratch on the door of the grand sitting room before she entered the dark chamber. Heavy mourning cloths covered all the windows, turning the bright yellow room into a dark, airless cave.

So, Her Grace feigns sorrow now.

She wondered if any true emotions ever penetrated the hard shell of the duchess's insufferable vanity. Clarinda, the Duchess of Gowdon, reclined in black furs and noir silks on her velvet chaise. A diamond of the first order since her triumphant first season, Her Grace still appeared as flawless and young as a debutante. Only now did Rosealise suspect how she maintained her luminous eyes, ghostly-pale complexion, and tiny waist.

Ignoring Rosealise, Clarinda nibbled on a strawberry with the indolence of a well-fed cat.

"Your Grace." She curtseyed. "I shall be leaving this morning on the Edinburgh coach."

The duchess arched a brow as she set aside a half-eaten berry, and then sipped from a crystal goblet. The murky wine it contained suggested a far less palatable tincture had been liberally added. If she was indulging in laudanum this early in the day, then Rosealise had the last of her proof. Clarinda had left London, bringing her young daughter to this remote Scottish estate, to conceal more than Mary's illness.

"Before I depart there is the matter of my unpaid wages, Your Grace," she said, keeping her tone carefully neutral. "I am owed ten pound sixpence."

"Our beloved child is dead." No matter what she said, Clarinda's voice held the sweet, high trill of a girl about to giggle. "You brought this dreadful disease into our household, Miss Dashlock. You sickened our poor, helpless Mary, and sent her to her grave. Now you demand wage for the horror you've visited upon us?"

Queen Victoria herself could not have

been more regally appalled. Rosealise briefly wondered what the penalty for slapping a duchess would be before she discarded the notion. If she were tossed into prison, she would not receive the help she now so desperately needed.

"You are mistaken, Your Grace," she said as civilly as she could. "When I entered your employ, you said nothing to me of Lady Mary's affliction. You bade me come to Scotland to look after a lively little girl. What I found on my arrival was a very sick child who could not rise from her bed. I came straight to you with the news. You claimed she had caught a chill."

The duchess selected another berry and examined it closely, as if it held more interest than Rosealise's recounting of the facts.

"That first night I also requested a doctor see to your daughter's care, as well as a nursemaid to stay with her at night. You refused me, and then forbid me from your presence." She paused for a moment to push back her anger, and then continued. "Weekly have I continued to beg for both. Since Mary's decline began last month, I did so daily. Your servants ignored me. You refused to respond to any of my notes."

"We recall no such communication." The duchess gave her the bland look she used instead of frowning. Turning the corners of one's mouth down created lines she didn't care to show on her pretty face. "We have had not a single note from you."

"I know you burned them," Rosealise told her. "When I tried to take Lady Mary to the village doctor myself, your servants took her from me. Your footmen locked me in my room. You forbid the coachmen to give me transport anywhere. I believe you also burned every letter I wrote to London, asking His Grace for help for Mary."

The duchess dropped the berry back on a plate, and then drained her goblet. "I remember these matters only vaguely. Some complaints, doubtless to cover your own culpability. We owe you nothing."

"How could you be so wicked?" Rosealise demanded. "She was a helpless child."

"You know nothing of me." Without warning Clarinda heaved the empty glass. "Get out."

Having some experience with the tantrums of nobility allowed Rosealise to nimbly dodge the crystal, which smashed on the marble floor behind her.

"I believe His Grace shall feel quite differently when I call on him in London," she said, freed now to pursue justice. "I will assure him of what I know to be true. He will make you answer for what you've done."

Clarinda sat up. "Do you think Gowdon will take your word over mine? You're nothing but a nameless, unwanted drab."

"You read far too many novels," Rosealise advised her. "The name Dashlock is very well known in Derbyshire. My mother was the daughter of a beloved vicar. My father was a decorated trooper of the Queen's Own Hussars, and became my grandfather's curate after the war. I have impeccable references from all of my former employers there and in London. You cannot sully my reputation with more of your lies, Madam."

"I am a Duchess," Clarinda said, coughing on her own title. She produced a small brown bottle and drank directly from it. "No one will believe you."

Doubtless she needed the opium tincture. Fever, blood loss and starvation had made the duchess quite beautiful. They also sped the progress of her affliction now.

"The handsome Scottish poet who spent so much time with you last winter recently died of consumption. So did your child. I expect so will I, in due time." Rosealise pointed at her. "You are the only connection we three share."

"Blue-stocking nonsense." The duchess surged to her feet, only to succumb to a longer fit of harsh, liquid coughing. The flecks of blood that stained her lips and hand had not yet turned dark red, as Mary's had in the last weeks of her life. "I will have you arrested for slander."

"I am proof of your sins." Although Rosealise wanted to feel pity for her, Clarinda hadn't sat for weeks holding a dying child's hand as she fought to breathe. "Whatever your husband decides to do with you, I have the comfort of knowing you will meet the same terrible end as your daughter and lover. Good-bye, Duchess."

Once she'd left the morning room, she

heard thumping and crashing sounds, but Rosealise didn't turn back. Picking up her case, she marched out of the castle and down the long drive to the road to watch for the coach to Edinburgh.

She felt sure that, once she spoke to the Duke, Gowdon would at the very least give her the unpaid wages. She'd need them for a doctor, and any treatment that might give her a little more time. Although she had always enjoyed good health, Rosealise did not feel especially optimistic.

She did have friends who cared for her, but she would not risk infecting them with the disease. Nor would she try to work as a governess again, as it would make her no better than Clarinda. The best she could hope for was to take a cottage in a small village where she might make lace or bonnets until the end came.

The coach arrived empty but for the driver, who clambered down to help her inside and stow her case.

"We'll be taking the back roads to Edinburgh, Miss," the driver said, and nodded toward a swath of black clouds brewing on the horizon. "Keep us clear of that joint-rattler."

She smiled and nodded, but once safely inside the carriage a strange depression sank into her. Trained for a lifetime in service, Rosealise had never expected to marry. Her excessive height and size usually repelled most men of her station. Losing her parents to cholera at such a young age made her decide never to have any of her own, which eliminated any other sort of romantic liaison. She had chosen to work as a governess because it suited her character, but also allowed her to exist on the fringes of her employers' families. The thought of dying didn't frighten her as much as the prospect of doing it in self-imposed solitude, like some scabrous leper.

I'll never be loved.

As the bumpy ride went on Rosealise's entrenched exhaustion persuaded her to fall into a light doze. She woke suddenly to a popping sound near her ear, and a terrible cursing issued from the driver. She leaned out to see the world gone dark, and terrible bolts of lightning crashing all around them. The horses screamed, and the coach suddenly jerked to one side. Rosealise smashed into the door, which flung open, hurling her out.

She tumbled roughly, heels over head, and felt her bones snapping. Her brow struck something so hard it cracked, and a warm wetness streaked down her face as she came to rest at the bottom of a muddy ditch.

When Rosealise opened her eyes, she stared into the wide, dead gaze of the driver. His body lay not a handspan from hers, crushed beneath part of his coach. The small hole in the front of his brow made it clear he'd been shot.

"Where she be?" a rough voice called out.

"Flattened under that, ye great dolt," another answered, and both men laughed.

After listening to the assassins depart on horses, Rosealise tried to crawl, but pain made her swoon. The thunder that later roused her boomed so loudly it made her sob with fear. She would drown in this ditch if she did not save herself, but she could not find the strength to move. She feared both of her legs had been broken, and her head hurt so much she almost wished to die.

Is this to be my end? This place, my grave?

Soft lavender light filtered into her blurred vision. A small figure descended from above, its pastel garments flowing like silk hair ribbons in a soft breeze. Rosealise gasped aloud as she saw it was a very small, young boy. He was so perfect in his countenance she felt sure she must be dreaming him. His pink wings fluttered gently as he landed beside her, and knelt down to look into her eyes. His tiny hand felt cold as he touched her face.

"My pet will be pleased. I hope he doesn't break you too quickly." He leaned closer. "You do love children. Perhaps we'll ravage you together."

Rosealise cowered from his words, as dreadful as his cold, clammy breath. She clumsily tried to roll away, but he held her down, incredibly strong for such a small, sweet boy, and rammed his little fingers into her chest.

❧

MAEL SEIZED Rosealise as they were flung through the burning light, and pressed her against him as it hurled them through an endless span of darkness. His senses became a jumble of confusion, and when he attempted to use his power to regain mastery of them, pain exploded inside his skull.

They landed on cold, hard rock, over which bands of color moved like blood spilled on dark flesh. Rosealise lay on his chest and over them curved the vague, rough dome of a cavern. All around them shards of stone drifted up, slowly rising as if the air had become water. The fragments expanded and shrank before gliding to the nearest rockface, into which they sank and vanished in a small burst of dust.

"Mael," Rosealise gasped. "I remember my life, all of it. I was a governess. My employer tried to have me killed, and then the Sluath found me." She pushed herself up from his chest, her eyes wide as she saw the strangeness of the rock. "Is this another trap?"

"No, lass." He knew this place of the damned, where he had sworn to end himself than ever chance returning. "'Tis where the Sluath made us slaves."

Chapter Thirty-One

S WALLOWED BY THE utter darkness of the demons' pit, Mael hung from his chains. Odorous muck surrounded him, but the stink of it no longer made him choke. Hunger gnawed at him, along with the endless burn of his rage, as hot and relentless as if his sire had chained him here. The despair that he would hang until he rotted from his shackles came and went, never permitted to linger long.

Since being made a Sluath slave he'd endured every torment, for Mael knew exactly why he'd been cast into the underworld.

'Tis what I've earned. 'Tis where I belong.

He heard a low cry, and the sound of something falling into the filth. A brief shower of light assured him that his tormentors had again returned to toy with him, but looking up blinded his dark-accustomed eyes. Before he could see clearly the light vanished.

The demons so loved their games. He'd been chained here for refusing to kill another captive. Yet if the wee fiend wished to make him fight another again, then he would allow the other slave to kill him. Death seemed a gift now, precious and coveted.

"Show yerself," he said, shouting the words. It had been so long since he'd spoken his voice rasped as badly as Broden's.

"I wish I could," a cool voice said, "but I fear I cannot find a candle to do so."

They'd thrown a woman in the pit with him. Did Meirneal think to make him end a helpless female?

A slender hand touched his leg. "Would you help me up, please, sir?"

"Aye, lass."

He grunted as he reached down for her, for his shackles had been locked tight, and the chains binding him to the side of the pit only stretched so far. Just as he thought his shoulders might pop out of their sockets, he grasped her hands, and tugged her to her feet.

As soon as he felt the softness of her skin and breathed in her scent he wondered if she had been sent as some new torment.

"I don't understand this." Her breath touched his mouth. "I suffered a dreadful accident, I think, and was badly hurt. Then I woke up here, which I cannot imagine the aftermath of such a thing. Where am I?"

She had been culled, Mael realized, like so many of the other slaves. Since being captured he had listened to many such whispered stories. He didn't want to tell her that she had been stolen from her time for the amusement of the cruelest beings ever created, but better that she know. Eventually the demons would come for her.

"'Tis the underworld," he said. "We're made slaves of the demons here."

Her hands tightened, and her body shivered. "Why?"

"I cannae tell ye that." Mael sighed. He knew exactly why he was here, but he couldn't speak of his own evil to such a lady. "Mayhap 'twill never be revealed to us."

"You must know something about these demons," she said.

"Naught ye'll wish to ken. Brace yerself now, lass," he said, stroking her back with what he hoped was a reassuring caress. "Demons stole ye from your time. Ye must have seen them. They've the visages of gods, and fly through the sky with wings. But they are as evil as nothing ye may imagine. They steal the souls of the helpless and the dying and bring them to this place. Here they torment us and use us for their own amusement."

"How long have you been down here?" She asked.

"I cannae tell ye." He wrapped his arms around her, hoping to give her some warmth. Her shivering had died away, and the desperate clutch of her hands no longer felt as tight. "Ye must be brave now."

☙❧

"I never ken a lady with your courage," Mael said, holding her waist as he helped her up from the hard stone. "I reckon 'tis why you seemed so familiar when you came to me at Dun Chaill."

"And you to me. Perhaps some part of me never forgot the man who gave me hope in that dreadful pit." Rosealise steadied herself with her hands on his arms, and looked around them. "This seems to be below ground, like the passage. Could it be that the underworld lies beneath the castle?"

"I dinnae ken." One of the floating stones puddled onto his arm like dirty water before sliding off and reforming into rock. "Wherever we've landed, 'tis enchanted by much magic."

She turned around. "I don't see an arch anywhere."

"Nor I." He caught her hand as she reached out to the nearest wall. "Permit me. I'm no' so easy to end."

"Touching the portal on the other side did make me feel as if I'd been burned," Rosealise said and touched her arm. As she watched him press his hand against the stone her mouth tightened. "The arch isn't there."

"Or 'tis concealed by spell again." Mael

inspected the wall before gazing at the others.
"I've no memory of these caves."

"I know who I am, who I was, but I still
don't recall a great deal about what
happened after I was stolen from my time,"
she admitted. "How did we move from that
disgusting pit to the chamber where they
confined us?"

"They took you from me." He tugged her
closer as writhing plants of a virulent orange
bloomed from the cave wall. "I thought they
meant to put you to torment. 'Tis what drove
me mad."

"Torment." She frowned. "You mean
torture? They tortured us?"

That she couldn't recall what the demons
had inflicted, Mael deemed a blessing.

"Dinnae dwell on what they did, lass."

Toothy holes appeared in the rock and
began to eat the wriggling blooms, which
spilled bright blue sap to run like blood down
the rough stone.

Rosealise shuddered. "I can well imagine
the Sluath calling this their home. It appears
as savage and baffling as the demons." She
winced and rubbed her temple.

"What more comes back to you?" he asked.

"I heard the small demon say that you broke free of your chains and climbed from the pit. He was the one called Meirneal." She went silent for a long moment. "I believe he'd taken me into a tall, narrow chamber filled with other demons. He was boasting of your escape to them, and...collecting on wagers, I think. They began to argue over what he called his winnings. While they were squabbling, I tried to creep away, but his guards caught and beat me." She regarded him. "What occurred during your escape? Did you find a passage out of here?"

Mael shook his head, and led her past the wall eating itself to another that seemed to be filling with scarlet snow.

"I ran through the tunnels searching for you, and the demons pursued me. When at last they struck me down, they dragged me in chains to where they had Broden." He wouldn't describe to her what they had been doing to the trapper, or how glad he had been to see Mael. "They bound me to a post, and gave him a spiked lash to flog me. When he refused, Meirneal threatened to cut both our throats. I bid him do it to save our hides."

"He had no choice but to whip you." Her eyes gleamed with new tears. "Oh, Mael. Now I understand why you called it torment."

"Aye," he said softly, "but they didnae only punish us."

❦

"Lout, Lout," Meirneal cooed as he skipped into the dismal chamber. "I've brought you a surprise."

Mael's chains rattled as he lifted his head, and the welts Broden had left on his back begin to bleed anew. The sight of the tiny, pretty fiend made his hands curl into fists, but he knew Meirneal would never come close enough for him to strike. He didn't bother to stand.

"I want naught from ye, Demon," he said, turning away.

"Don't mope about the whipping. Your handsome comrade did such splendid work, and never shed a tear for you. Seabhag was moved to reward him." The little Sluath capered around him and grinned. "Since your escape brought me that which I greatly desired, you will also benefit." He snapped his fingers, and two more demons came in, dragging the bedraggled, mud-splattered body of a fair-haired female between them. "Under all that mush she's very fresh."

Mael had never seen her, but he recognized the scent that came from her. She smelled as sweet and fresh as she had in the pit.

"You don't seem very pleased, Lout," Meirneal said. "Only look at how large she is. A true match for you, don't you think? Sturdy bones, too. She's unlikely to break as quickly as the others we time-culled." He gestured for the demons to bring the female closer. "See how well she took her first punishment?"

Mael felt a terrible pity as they dropped the lady across his legs. She had been badly beaten, her long, mud-caked curls only veiling the cuts and bruises marring her lovely face. Dried blood hemmed the inside curves of her lips, which had split. He looked up at the small demon, and in that moment knew hatred that not even Fargas had inspired in his heart.

"Why did ye beat her?" he demanded.

The demon giggled. "Because, silly, tearing out her throat would have only pleasured me."

"Take her back from whence ye found her," Mael said, unable to resist resting his palm on her soft curls. "I'll do as ye bid."

"You'll do that anyway, once I've finished with you. Now, you'll want to scrub off the mud before you amuse yourself with her." Meirneal moved his hands, and Mael's cell transformed from an empty box of blood-spattered stone to a beautiful chamber filled with artful furnishings and tables laden with rich foods. A marble fountain bubbled beside a large white tub of steaming water. "Or not, if you prefer your whores earthy. Many of your sort do."

"She's no' mine," Mael countered.

"Exactly, but I am lending her to you for now." He bared twin rows of tiny, sharp teeth. "I suggest you use the hottest water. It eliminates the need to scrub, and I do like how rosy pink they turn after a scalding. It makes them feel every bite more keenly."

Mael glanced down at the heavy chains

confining him. "Aye, and how am I to bathe her, then? With my hopes?"

"You have no more hope, Lout. You wouldn't be here if you did." The little demon skipped back across the room, pausing on the threshold before he flicked power at Mael, freeing him from his shackles. "Use her as much as you like. Do whatever you wish to her. Pretend she's me."

Meirneal's laughter echoed as soon as the door closed and vanished, and Mael lifted the lass in his arms, intent on carrying her over to the huge bed.

Cool gray eyes peered up at him. "Be advised, sir, that any attempt by you to molest my person will be met with violent resistance."

It was the same voice he'd heard in the darkness. He stopped and gently lowered her onto her feet, spreading his hands to show her he meant no harm.

"I shallnae force myself on ye, lass. I'm no' a brute or a demon."

"I can see that much." She shook out her long black skirt and then gathered her hair, coiling and tying it into a large knot behind her head. Although she moved carefully, she showed no sign of discomfort. "You were captured by these creatures, as I was?"

"Aye." She seemed to have no memory of him, and he had no wish to remind her of the pit. "They took us to serve as slaves."

"Oh, I think not. Slavery is against the law." She regarded the interior of his cell for some time before she met his gaze. She seemed uncomfortable. "I regret there is no one here to introduce us properly. I am Miss Rosealise Dashlock of London, England." She extended her hand with the palm to the side.

He'd never met a female with so lengthy a name, but he guessed she wished to clasp hands in a like manner that warriors did with their arms.

"Mael mag Raith."

As he touched his palm to hers, a sparkling warmth spread over his fingers and moved up into his arm.

"I am pleased to make your acquaintance, Mr. Raith." Her mouth curved slightly. "I do hope we may become good friends as we endeavor to regain our freedom." She glanced down at her mud-streaked skirt. "First I think I should have a wash."

THE NEEDLING PAIN in Rosealise's head eased away as her recollection abruptly ended.

"I wish I could recall more, but my memory remains in shards. I think we should not linger here, either, else the demons find us." She saw three shadowed openings in the cave walls. "Which tunnel should we follow?"

Mael studied each before nodding toward the center. "That one branches off in many directions we might quickly take to elude the demons."

She took hold of his hand. "Then shall we push onward, my titan?"

The center tunnel appeared shrouded in darkness from afar, but as they walked to it the outlandish lights and colors moving on the stone walls seemed to accompany them. Rosealise tried not to stare at the bizarre forms they shaped, but some astounded her.

A coach made of severed heads driven by a headless man rushed past her, pulled by four skeletons of horses. Beside Mael huge gray boars with bloodied tusks marched like soldiers, complete with ancient Roman armor.

Over their heads swans fashioned of golden gears and ivory fangs gnashed on each other as they flew from one side of the cave to the other. When one dropped to attack Mael, it flew at his head and then through it, chewing furiously as it hurtled back up to the others.

"'Tis but illusions," he murmured to her. "Naught can harm us."

When they stepped into the tunnel, she glanced back to see the entire cave go dark while the bizarre wraiths poured into the walls of the tunnels. "The magic in this place moves with us."

Mael nodded. "'Tis part of the torment-ing, I reckon." He stopped and peered ahead of them. "We're close to the center, where they abide. Keep silent from here, lass."

Rosealise gripped his hand more tightly, and tried to ignore the illusion of glowing purple vultures lunging out of the wall to snap at her face. She was perilously close to swooning with hysterics, which would not do.

The end of the long passage opened into another cavern so large that Rosealise couldn't see the opposite side. Tall, narrow, sharp-peaked structures unlike any she'd ever seen stretched from the cave floor to the high ceiling. Sluath glyphs covered the toothy buildings, lending them a mottled look. She saw no windows, doors or any manner in which they could be entered.

The air smelled strangely tainted, as if something huge lay rotting in a stagnant pond.

The stone vault above the structures held crude chandeliers of stone thickly encrusted with dull-looking amber crystals. Large spheres that looked the same floated over a giant bridge fashioned from ice or glass. It stretched from the near side of the cavern, arching upward, before disappearing in the distance. Below it two great black circles hovered, connected by a thin stream of clouds that seemed frozen in motion.

Staring at the cloud stream made Rosealise's stomach shrivel.

Only when she gazed around the very perimeter of the enormous cave did she finally see the unmoving figures. None of them appeared to be demons. Instead they were statues of people, hundreds of them, hewn from a pale, gleaming stone. Each had been dressed in actual garments of a bewildering

assortment and deplorable state. Ancient
soldiers in blood-stained kilts stood aside ladies
in ball gowns tattered to ribbons. There were
primitives in scabby furs who stared blindly at
nobility in threadbare velvet. Many held large
stones in their battered hands. Some pushed
carts piled high with crystals. Terrible wounds
and bruises mottled the faces and limbs of all
the statues, as if the sculptor had wished to
make them all appear on the brink of being
worked to death.

Mael moved silently as he guided her from
one position of hiding to another, until they
drew close to one of the statues. That was
when Rosealise saw a Roman's eyes shift
toward them, proving they weren't statues
at all.

These were the slaves of the Sluath, left
frozen in their tracks by their masters.

Chapter Thirty-Two

D OMNALL WALKED THE length of the buttery again and again, moving his torch from side to side as he inspected every inch of the windowless chamber. No sign of any disturbance had appeared, yet the old floor stones looked as clean as if scrubbed.

"Like the passage to the tower," he said to Jenna. "'Tis been scoured."

"It was still dirty last night. We were going to sweep it out today, after Rosealise showed me how to make some straw brooms." His wife wrapped her arms around her waist. "She couldn't have done all this by herself last night."

"Chieftain," Edane said as he came in

from the old pantry. "I found a wash basin overturned in Mael's chamber. Water yet darkens the floor stones. He left his tartan draped on the bed, over this." He exchanged a look with Jenna as he held out the map scroll.

Domnall took it from him. "Mael wouldnae keep this in his chamber. What more?"

"Naught." The archer's expression turned sheepish. "Mayhap the lady chose to walk outside with Mael, and they, ah, became diverted by personal matters."

"For the entire night, with the Sluath out there, possibly hunting us again?" Jenna countered. "They wouldn't be that stupid."

"Aye, and Mael wouldnae keep the lady out to slumber in the cold." Domnall heard voices coming from the kitchens and strode out.

"No fresh tracks outside the keepe," Broden said as soon as he saw them. "I've no' Mael's skill, but he leaves the largest, deepest prints. 'Twould be impossible to miss if he crossed soil."

"My hunters saw no trace in the forests or by the stream," Kiaran added. "The mound remains empty. No sign in the gardens and maze."

Domnall felt again the weight of unseen eyes, and made an old hand signal by his side that the men and Jenna saw.

"Mayhap they didnae leave Dun Chaill in the night," Edane said suddenly, and scowled at the trapper. "Another trap may yet hold them. One that eluded you whilst you wasted your night preening."

"More likely they sought a private spot to share," Broden said, his voice flinty, "and yet dinnae wish to be found. No' that your worth-less magic could trace them."

"Traps don't dump water basins or scrub floors, Edane." Jenna faced the trapper. "And you're the reason Rosealise and Mael aren't sharing anything right now, pretty boy." When the archer chuckled she turned on him. "You think it's funny? Really? If they're in trouble, we're all they've got." She glared at the trap-per. "Do *not* make this about you two and your incessant crap."

Both men muttered, "Aye, my lady" and stared at their boots.

Domnall touched his wife's shoulder,

admiring her show of temper. "'Twill be well, *luaidh*." To Broden and Kiaran he said, "Walk the passages again. Seek even the smallest change in what you ken of the stronghold. Dinnae risk yourselves, but make note of the place and return to the hall. We'll consult the scroll."

Kiaran nodded and left with Broden.

After making a point to check the stones that still blocked off the chamber of iron warriors, Domnall spread out the map on the trestle table where a large patch of sunlight fell on the wood. As he did, Edane moved slowly around him and Jenna, leaning over to inspect the scroll as he muttered under his breath. When at last the archer came to stand between them, he continued examining the map.

"We cannae be heard now outside the spell circle I cast," Edane said, "but we may be yet seen. 'Twill last until one of us crosses the circle. Behave as if naught has changed."

"Sorry I was so mean to you," Jenna said as she pointed at the center of the map. "Look, here's absolutely nothing important, so it looks like we're talking about the scroll. I thought Broden's bit about your magic being worthless was inspired." She frowned at Domnall. "How long do we have to keep up this act, my love?"

"Until we find the watcher," Domnall told her. "The falconer now patrols the stronghold through the eyes of his birds They'll each hover over different parts of the keepe while we make the pretense of searching again for traps. When the watcher again moves through the passages, Kiaran shall map his path."

Setting tracking spells inside Dun Chaill last night had required Edane and Broden to work together while staying far apart. After the evening meal Edane had gone to the mound on pretense of retrieving more iron, and there cast his spell over a clutch of rocks too small to be easily noticed. Kiaran had acted as go-between, carrying back the archer's bespelled stones to the trapper, who had surreptitiously placed them around the stronghold while delivering fire wood for the hearths. While they slept the watcher had triggered but one spell stone that had been left in Mael's chamber, but it was enough to confirm the chieftain's suspicions.

Domnall's one regret was that none of them had noticed his tracker and the English-woman had gone missing until the morning meal.

"I hope he makes a move soon." Jenna leaned against him, and as he bent his head to kiss her, she asked, "My measurements tell me that there are a lot of internal spaces in this place. What if he's got Rosealise and Mael chained up between the walls somewhere?"

"Then we shall tear down the facking walls," he murmured against her brow.

Jenna looked up at him, a new light in her eyes. "Or I walk through them."

Chapter Thirty-Three

S EEING HOW THE Sluath had left their slaves sickened Mael, but it explained how the demons kept the mortals imprisoned even in their absence. He wondered if the same had been done to him and the other Mag Raith after their capture. Too much of his past still lay maddeningly just out of reach of memory.

"Can we free them?" Rosealise said, and reached out toward the Roman. Sparks burst near her fingertips, which she snatched away. "It burns, like the stone in the underground tower passage."

"'Tis been bespelled against other mortals." When he tried to put his hand on the frozen slave, something unseen pushed his hand away. "And immortals. We cannae free them, my lady."

"We cannot leave them like this."

Before she could say more, she coughed into her hand. As the spate worsened, she began to shake.

Mael lifted her into his arms and carried her away from the Roman to a large, flat stone. As soon as they drew near, it filled with light and changed its form. He stopped and looked down at the curved wooden bench, and prodded the long, tufted cushion atop it with his boot toe. It felt as it looked, but he took the precaution of setting down Rosealise before he perched on it.

"This was Her Grace's divan," she said as he drew her down beside him, and at his frown she added, "It belonged to the duchess who tried to kill me." She covered her mouth again and cleared her throat. "How can it be here? Why would the Sluath have it?"

As Rosealise took her hand away he saw the smear of blood on her fingers. "Likely the demons stole it when they took you. We'll rest here until you feel stronger."

"That's unlikely, my dear sir," she said, a

troubling rasp roughening her voice. "In the end the disease that Her Grace inflicted on me will snuff out my life. There is no escaping my death."

He thought of his sire, whom he was sure had not lived to a great age. Fargas's love of drink and brawls had already ruined his body, and his health would have followed next.

"Aye, but some may dodge the end for a time, if the Gods are stirred to intervene."

"The Gods, sir?" Rosealise said softly. "I cannot believe they would send the Sluath after me."

His lady knew he carried great guilt, but not the reason for it. They might never escape the underworld and find their way back to Dun Chaill. If by some miracle they did, he owed the Mag Raith the truth. For now, he would entrust it to Rosealise.

"I cannae make such a claim. In truth I brought the wrath of the Gods down on myself and all my brothers. 'Twas my evil that drew the Sluath to us, and damned the Mag Raith for eternity."

"Though I would never attempt to persuade you to tell me of it," she said as she tucked her arm through his. "I would hear it all if it could lighten your heart."

"'Tis time you ken." He brought her hand to his mouth and kissed it before he rose from the divan. Looking upon the Sluath's world brought back all the misery of his own mortal life. "On that day we were taken, I'd schemed to murder a man that night."

"You?" she said, her eyebrows arching. "You killed someone?" When he shook his head, her brow furrowed. "How can you be evil for thinking of it?"

"'Twas but by chance I didnae carry out my plan," Mael told her. "Had we returned from our last hunt I wouldnae have rested until his blood lay on my hands. Such rage I felt, I ken naught could stop me."

Coldness crept into his voice as he told her of the brute Fargas had been, and how Mael had been prevented by tribal law from protecting his family against his sire. He recounted how Fargas's violence had grown worse with drink, until the night when his sire had lost what little control he'd had. Seeing his mother and youngest sister with broken bones had decided everything for Mael.

"I saw then that 'twouldnae end until they died at my sire's hand." He looked down at his own, so like his sire's he often wished he could hack them from his wrists. "While Fargas slept I took my *máthair* and sisters to the shaman, and bid him keep them safe. When I returned to our *broch*, I emptied all my sire's jugs of drink. I waited until he roused, and told him he'd drained them dry. In that time, he often did, so he believed me. I then vowed to trade game for more drink if he went with me on a night hunt. 'Twas all lies, but I didnae care."

Rosealise sighed. "That isn't evil, my dear sir."

"I lied about more than the drink, lass," Mael admitted. "The pig I meant to hunt, 'twas Fargas. I schemed to lead him to a high cliff, snap his neck, and push him over the edge. None would be the wiser. 'Twould look as if he'd fallen. I could return to the tribe and care for my family, and he would never again harm them."

❦

ROSEALISE HAD no doubt he would have

indeed murdered Fargas. She also had no doubt that doing so was the only way Mael could have saved his mother and sister. She heard that truth in every word he spoke. But his confession provided a painful clarity to his shame. He believed that just the thought damned him just as much as if he had done the thing. Few would understand, much less forgive, a son intent on killing his own father —unless they knew the lifetime of witnessing and suffering violence that Mael had experienced at Fargas mag Raith's hands.

"The evil came from your father," she said firmly. "Not you."

His mouth twisted. "You cannae blame Fargas for the evil in my heart."

"He inflicted it," she insisted. "Fargas gave you no other direction to take. Your tribe stood by and did nothing. Your mother and sisters could not fight him. You were not permitted to take them away from him. Only ending his life could put a stop to his brutality, and save your family."

Mael averted his gaze. "'Twas the path I chose to take."

"I'll guess that you never thought of

murdering Fargas until he showed you the depth of the true evil in him." She nodded at his startled look. "What you intended for your father didn't come from hatred. You wished to protect a helpless woman and her children. In the end, my dear sir, you couldn't carry out your plans. You condemn yourself for something that you never did?"

"It sprang from a heart gone dark and evil," he insisted. "'Tis proof that I'm the worst of men."

"I could not care for such a gentleman," Rosealise assured him. "Since I love you, I know you are mistaken."

"I've ever loved you, from the moment you fell from the sky." He closed his eyes. "But it doesnae redeem me."

She suddenly knew how to address his shame. "You and your clan fight the Sluath because they stole our lives from us, and tried to make us their slaves. Jenna told me that Domnall even slew the one who struck her down when you first came to Dun Chaill. Do you think your chieftain evil for what he did? Is he damned because he ended the life of that scout, who would surely have killed you

all if he had not? Should Domnall die
for it?"

"No," he said flatly. "The scout was
a demon."

"Yes." She beckoned him to her, and when
he crouched in front of her she touched his
cheek. "Just as Fargas was."

Mael closed his eyes, his shoulders hunch-
ing. As a terrible, wrenching groan came from
his chest, Rosealise felt her thigh burn, and
saw the glyphs on her lover's arm paling from
black to silver. She slipped off the divan and
clasped him in her arms. Holding him,
stroking his back and making low, comforting
sounds as he released all the grief inside him
was all she could offer, but he needed
only that.

In this place of despair and enslavement,
her lover had finally freed himself.

Chapter Thirty-Four

THE BRIGHTNESS OF the midday sun warmed Galan's shoulders, but he kept his hood over his head to protect his eyes. Since coming to the village, he had taken to spending his nights awake and slumbering from dawn to dusk. Another curious effect had provided far more pleasure for him, but that discovery Galan had kept to himself.

The Sluath, he discovered, had no need for sleep, although they all chose to withdraw into darkness every few nights. The utter absence of light seemed important to this ritual, as did distance from the village. He yearned to know what they did once so separated from the others, but thus far had not been able to observe a demon in such sequestration. He suspected it had something to do with maintaining their glamor, which brightened and became more detailed each time they returned from their solitary retreats.

Now he walked along the row of bespelled mortals dressed in clean if shabby garments. Carefully he checked each face and body for any flaw that might betray their true purpose. The magic that Prince Iolar had used on them had erased the physical signs of the plague, lending them the appearance of healthy, well-fed villagers.

Like all the others they had sent out to hunt the Mag Raith, they had been commanded to plead for help with a badly-injured druid they would describe as Galan. They would then lead the hunters back to the village, where sentries posted in the slopes would signal their approach. The demons had restored the village entirely, making it appear as it had been before the plague and the Sluath occupation. Domnall and his men would never suspect what hid in the cottages until it was too late for them to run.

Galan stopped before one young farmer with red hair, whose wasted muscles now appeared robust and powerful.

"This one trembled on the edge of death no' twoday past," he called out to the prince's second. "How long shall he live on?"

Danar came to inspect the mortal. "His veins darken, and his flesh yellows. His organs will fail by week's end."

Galan gestured for the farmer to step out of line. "Take him to the barn and bind him in the loft," he told the big demon's guards.

Danar said nothing more until they finished their inspection and sent the bespelled mortals on their way. When Galan started for the barn and the delights that awaited him there, however, the demon clamped a heavy hand on his neck.

"If you think to put that mortal to some other purpose," the big demon said, "be sure it will not deny our prince his nightly pleasures."

Since Iolar had killed off all of the villagers without plague he had been taking the sick ones and transforming them for his sport. When his ghastly games made the cries of the suffering mortals so loud Galan was obliged to ward the prince's cottage to stifle the noise. He had resented that as well as the waste of flesh, until he'd walked in on the prince in the midst of toying with a dying mortal.

That night had proven most enlightening.

"I but test on them how I shall persuade the Pritani shaman to open the underworld gate," he assured Danar. Telling a half-truth, Galan had learned, deceived the demons when a lie could not. "He'll be returned to the slave pens when I'm finished."

Though Danar released him, Galan still felt the weight of the Sluath's gaze on his back. The demon could prove nothing, of course. Thanks to Iolar's power, Galan always returned the mortals he used without a trace of what he did to them in the loft.

Once inside the barn he bolted the doors and removed his hooded cloak. As he walked toward the ladder hanging from the upper level, he flicked his fingers at the lanterns, extinguishing their lights. The cool comfort of darkness accompanied him up to the small loft, where the guards had left the farmer bound to the roof post.

Lack of light hid the mortal's face like a black mask, also helpful to Galan's aim. He walked up to the younger man, testing the feel of his thick hair. This one could be compelled to braid strands of it, as some of the others had, but he was too impatient to wait for a more convincing façade. He also hated that he could not pluck what he wanted from the mortal's mind, as the Sluath did. He removed his dagger, plying the very edge of the blade against the farmer's mouth.

"Do you fear this blade, lad?"

"Aye." The man spoke without emotion, but he shivered slightly.

"Do not move." He had to be careful not to cut off the lips this time, Galan thought, and sent a surge of power through the dagger. "You're named Edane."

"I'm Edane." The lie came easily, as Galan already had him completely under his spell.

He traced the tip of the blade down over the farmer's chin and rested it in the hollow of his throat. Soon he'd have the real Pritani shaman at his mercy, but for now, this sham-Edane would have to do.

Galan leaned closer, and put his lips against the mortal's ear, licking the lobe before he said, "Tell me of your most dire fear."

Chapter Thirty-Five

MAEL WOULD HAVE happily remained in Rosealise's arms until the underworld crumbled around them. Yet they had to find their way back to Dun Chaill before the Sluath returned, or face enslavement again. He also heard her breath grow shallower, and knew she was trying not to cough.

"We must try again to find the portal in the tunnels," he said as he rose and helped her to her feet. "Can you walk that far?"

Though she nodded and smiled, her throat moved as she swallowed several times.

As they passed the frozen slaves Mael looked into their eyes, which yet moved, and saw how they turned from side to side. He'd seen that motion before, beneath the eyelids of his sleeping sisters.

"I dinnae reckon they see us," he told his lady as he guided her toward the tunnel entry. "Their eyes move as when mortals sleep."

She glanced at the Roman they had first seen. "Surely the Sluath can't make them dream." She stopped and tugged on his arm. "I understand now. The duchess's divan...they didn't steal it from her castle. The stone took it from my memories when I drew near."

"'Tis using our thoughts to shape itself," he agreed. He turned to the nearest stone wall, and took a step closer to it. Light and color poured over the rock, changing it into a tall hedge of brambles with blood-red thorns. "The maze in the garden at Dun Chaill, but I didnae think of the place."

"Nor did I once recall Her Grace's furnishings." Rosealise thought for a moment. "The maze at Dun Chaill tried to kill us. The duchess did the same to me just before the Sluath captured me. These illusions do not use ordinary thoughts or memories. I remember now. They prey on that which we fear."

Chapter Thirty-Six

✦

A S THE FULL bloom of the warm spring had given way to the sweet grasses of summer, Jenna's hope had faded like the garden. Hardly pausing on her usual walk, she stooped and gathered some sprigs of pastel purple heather and the drooping bluebells that matched them. As she passed the outer wall and made for the hedge maze, her feet found their way along the trodden down path they'd made.

What would Mael and Rosealise think if they could see me?

Rosealise would likely have to laugh at the skirt.

Left with a mound of tartans brought from the cache, but without the Englishwoman's seemingly endless knowledge of the domestic arts, Jenna had felt obliged to at least try her hand at sewing. The hem was longer in back than in front, the seams between the panels were unraveling at an alarming rate, and there wasn't a single straight line in sight—anywhere. The men had certainly not clamored for her sewing skills. In fact she'd had the distinct impression that their faces turned away to hide smirks.

If she and her skirt could help to lighten the mood, then it was worth it.

But as always when she approached the small stone altar that Broden had made, her own mood sobered. A flat piece of gray slate was supported by two others that stood vertical, their bottoms rammed into the earth just outside the maze entrance. She brushed aside the withered remains of last week's flowers. Though she'd given up on the formal prayers early on, she silently sent her usual entreaty to the Gods of her highlanders.

Since the guys think you're out there, how about proving them right? All you have to do is send Rosealise and Mael back to us.

Silence, as usual, was the only answer—not that it surprised her.

Maybe it was her imagination, but she'd recently noticed that the men seemed to mention the Gods less of late. One by one they had finally had to admit that Mael and Rosealise were gone. The frantic searching of the first few days had turned to staring at the sky during storms, but eventually the weeks had dragged by. Though Jenna had only known Rosealise for days, the bond they'd forged in the underworld had been strong. It also surprised her how much she'd liked having another woman in the keepe.

With a sigh, Jenna lay the new flowers next to Edane's candle.

As much as she missed Rosealise, the men had suffered worse. Each had dealt with the loss of their brother in their own way.

Domnall had worked ceaselessly to make Dun Chaill safer for them all, adding his own marks to the map that Rosealise had found.

After complaining that a memorial was something that Mael wouldn't have wanted, Broden had helped her build the altar anyway. She noticed that he'd taken great care to dress the edges of the slate beautifully. When it was finished, he'd crossed his arms and looked down at it, but nodded before he left.

Edane and Broden had stopped their bickering almost immediately. It was as if they'd realized that even an immortal brother might be lost. Edane had brought so many candles to accompany her flowers, that concentric, puddled rings of melted wax covered almost the entire surface of the top slate.

But it was the falconer that most worried Jenna. Kiaran had yet to say Mael's name.

The ink along her spine began to tingle and warm just as footfalls sounded behind her. Jenna smiled as Domnall's big arms wound around her. She pressed her back against the hard muscles of his chest and hugged his arms closer to her. This was something new as well. Domnall found all manner of reasons to seek her out during the day.

"I've brought your fresh eggs to the kitchens," he said, nuzzling behind her ear. His warm breath on the back of her neck tickled. "Tell me again the name of that dish of yours."

When she tried to turn to him, he held her in place and nuzzled behind her other ear.

"Frittata," she said, wriggling a little, "and it's not really mine."

Though she'd done frightfully little cooking in her time as an architect and even less during school, she'd learned a few simple things that had kept her from starving.

Rosealise had probably known so much more.

As though he'd heard her thoughts, he said, "Mael 'twould be better with the chickens. He kens the ways of the animals from all his tracking."

Jenna managed to turn around, looked up into Domnall's lean face, and laid her hands along both sides of it.

"I love that you never speak about them in the past," she said.

"For they arenae," he declared.

"Simple as that?" she said, as she placed her hands on his chest.

"Naught 'tis simple about the Sluath." He pulled her closer. "But aye, 'tis something deep in my bones." He gazed steadily into her eyes. "I ken you feel it too."

Jenna thought for a long moment and

glanced back at the altar. The couple's disap-
pearance had left a cavernous hole in everyone's lives, yes. The clan all grieved in their
own ways. But even now, after all this time, she
somehow couldn't give up the hope that
Rosealise and Mael weren't really gone.

As she turned back to Domnall to tell him
so, he lightly kissed her forehead and tucked
her against his side. Without another word,
and with his arm around her waist, they
started back up the path.

Chapter Thirty-Seven

ROSEALISE COULDN'T HOLD back the cough that came then, or the blood that filled her mouth. She fell to her knees, coughing out as much as she could before she dragged in a shallow breath. Her chest felt as if she were gulping water instead of air.

When she could get enough to speak, she said, "Could you take my arm, my dearest love?"

Mael did more than that and carried her into the tunnel, where the stone walls illuminated with caricatures of herself. She saw herself dying, dead, and rotting. On one narrow ledge the duchess, now a skeleton in fine black silk, leered down at her as she pointed a pistol at Rosealise's head. Yet as Rosealise stared back, thinking only of the love she had found with Mael twice now in the underworld, the illusion turned to dark green smoke and vanished. In its place the happy face of Mary, the duchess's daughter, swam into view.

Miss Dashlock! I've missed you so! I know it's frightfully selfish of me, but I can hardly wait to see you again. Such happy days.

Rosealise reached out a trembling hand to the smiling child. It wasn't the pain of her lingering death that little Mary remembered— it was the love. But just as their fingers were about to touch, Mary shimmered brightly, then faded away.

This is what the demons are hiding from us.

"Mael," she gasped, "look."

As a sharp pain lanced through her chest, she remembered with utter clarity how they could leave this place.

BUT MAEL DIDN'T NEED to be told. An army of pig-headed brutes had pursued him down the tunnel, but as Rosealise's breathing had become shallower, he clutched her tighter. Naught would stop him from finding a way out and giving her breath some ease. He hadn't found her in the underworld twice only to lose her this soon.

"Hold on, my love," Mael said, his words turning the pig army into hundreds of tendrils of dark green smoke that wafted away.

In their place he saw the lovely, smiling faces of his family, who now gathered like wraiths before him. He smiled back, astonished to see how tall and beautiful his young sisters had grown. His mother's hair had gone white, but her face radiated quiet joy. She reached out to him, her slender hand marked with a bent reed, the mark given to a widow of the tribe. His sire had died, and not by his hand.

Ye saved us, lad. I but wish we might have done the same for ye. Someday shall we see ye again, my son.

Relief flooded through him and in that moment all came back. Mael knew how they could return to Dun Chaill.

"The bridge," he said, just as Rosealise rasped, "I remember."

∞❧∞

PEERING THROUGH THE DARKNESS, Rosealise saw the small flare of light at the other end of the tunnel.

"They've given the signal," she murmured to the others before she looked at her lover. "Are you quite prepared for this, my titan?"

Mael brought her hand to his lips. "Aye, my *jem*."

He wrapped his hand around hers, and quickly hurried with her through the passage. At the other end Domnall stood waiting to operate the mechanism that opened the storm stream.

"Mael first, and then you, Dash," he said as he grasped the lever. He looked worried, but then he always did. "Never two together."

Rosealise nodded. The demon had told them that if two went together, they would die.

"Thank you, dear friend," she replied.

She turned to face her lover. Looking into his eyes wrenched at her heart, but she would be strong for him now.

"I adore you, you know. You're the kindest, gentlest soul I've ever known. If we survive this, I will be your wife and have your children and exasperate you for the rest of our days." Or love him for as long as her consumption would allow, she added silently but honestly in her head.

"I shall find you again," he declared.

Mael held her with the hard desperation of a man about to leap through time to an unknown destination. He lingered with her a moment longer, and then climbed up to the sky bridge.

Rosealise had to blink back tears as she watched the cloaked demon guide him to the proper spot, and then lean close for a final confidence. When he jumped and disappeared into the cloud stream a wretched cry spilled from her lips.

"Dash," Domnall said. When she met his gaze, his stern expression softened. "'Twillnae be for naught. I vow it."

"I will hold you to that pledge, Hunter."

She went over to kiss his cheek before she made her way up to the bridge. There the demon took her hand, filling her with calm, and accompanied her to the edge. Looking down brought another surge of fear, so Rosealise looked instead into the demon's eyes.

"Thank you, my dear," Rosealise said. "I fear I can never repay you for what you've done for us."

"Someday you shall," the demon promised, and then touched her brow with cold fingers. "Until you find your love again, recall nothing of yourself or this."

She fell into a strange, soft grayness that made leaping into the stream a simple business. As the wind whirled her out into the darkness of the storm, Rosealise's last thought was of that strange, large man with the jewel-like eyes, whose name she could no longer remember.

Chapter Thirty-Eight

CUL TILTED HIS head as he heard the thump of boots over it. He'd sealed the hatch in the tower base weeks past, so he had no fear at being discovered. The hunters had searched every inch of the castle looking for their seneschal and his lover, to no avail. Even the chieftain's wife, who used her power to shift into wraith form and walk through walls, had found nothing.

Diverting Jenna away from the parts of Dun Chaill Cul reserved for his own use had been simple. Although she didn't realize it, using her power made her vulnerable to his own.

Less gratifying was Prince Iolar's refusal to

leave the mortal village he occupied. While Cul had kept careful watch, the demons remained obstinately entrenched, sending out only a handful of bespelled mortals every few days. The humans all scattered in different directions, as if performing reconnaissance for their masters. Cul had been tempted to kill the two who strayed too close to his castle. Fortunately, they had wandered into the lower ridges, disturbing a large herd of red hinds that had trampled them to death.

Cul suspected the druid had convinced the Sluath of some new scheme to open the gates. He would be stupid enough to use mortal scouts, of course. As for the demons, the longer they remained in the mortal realm, the more they would suffer as he had. Soon nothing but a return to the underworld would restore them—and then he would drop the spell protecting Dun Chaill, and lure them to the only gate left open.

Chapter Thirty-Nine

MORE BLOOD WELLED up from Rosealise's wheezing lungs. Mary had died in this fashion, bewildered and yet courageous to the very end. She could be brave about it too. But she couldn't avoid breathing the tainted air of the underworld, which added another twisting knife inside her chest.

"Almost there," Mael told her.

As they approached the bridge and passed the lever, she saw him release it despite the fact that her vision was dimming. She spat out dark red blood and felt her head whirl.

"You first, lass," he said, and she felt him bend down.

We are going home now, my titan, but I will not go alone.

As he set her gingerly on her feet, still supporting her weight, her knees wobbled and blood trickled down from the side of her mouth.

"The Gods 'twill give you safe landing," he whispered, holding her to his chest. "Or they must answer to me. I pray your breathing 'twill be easier, as 'twas before." He kissed her forehead. "I shall find you again."

But if there was one thing Rosealise could not abide, it wasn't how she could no longer draw a breath. It was being separated from the man she loved. She could not risk landing in a different time, no matter the cost. Here at the end, being with him was all that mattered.

We began this journey together, my titan, and that is how it will finish. We will not surrender. We will take our love back to our friends, and our home.

His arms let go of her, and she tipped slowly backward. But as the underworld started to go dark, Rosealise used the last shred of her strength. She flung her arms around Mael's neck and pulled him over the side of the bridge with her.

"Rosealise!" Mael exclaimed as he clutched her, their bodies spinning as the cloud stream caught them.

The storm rushed over her face, dragging her hair toward the floating black oval. As it swallowed her and Mael, Rosealise felt her heart go still.

Wherever it took them, whatever death brought, in Mael's arms she was already home.

⚜

WATER PATTERED atop Mael's head, sliding down over his face. It was warm and soft, as tears from the Gods might be. He could feel that he sat against a hard stone wall, and held a long, slender shape of a woman in his arms. Both of them wore nothing but their flesh. When he opened his eyes, he saw sunlight glowing on a sopping wet mane of pale gold curls, but it still took him a moment to remember her name.

"Rosealise."

His voice sounded worse than Broden's, but at least this time she would know it to be him. When she didn't move or reply he swept back her hair and saw the tracks of dark blood running down her throat. No breath came from her, and the terrible stillness of her face had gone chalk-white. Raindrops fell on her delicate skin causing the blood to run in small rivulets.

There is no escaping my death, she had said.

"You cannae do thus, my lady." He brought her closer, holding her against him and resting his cheek against her hair. "'Tisnae time for you to go away from me. We've the rest of spring, and summer, and fall, and I shall have them with you."

"Is that...*Mael?*"

He heard Jenna's voice as if from a great distance, but paid it no heed. Holding Rosealise to his heart and feeling the roar of pain billowing in his chest became his universe. When someone touched him, he jerked away, protecting his lady with his body hunched over hers. But finally he let out the howl of grief, and felt the stones shake behind his back.

Something cool caressed his face, but this time it didn't feel wet. It felt like Rosealise's touch. The lips that brushed against his tasted of his lady.

He'd gone mad, Mael decided, almost relieved by the prospect. He felt sorry for the Mag Raith, who would have to end him. That, or he'd spend the rest of eternity holding a corpse and believing it alive.

"I would never be so bold as to kiss a stranger," a brisk voice said, whispering warm breath against his cheek. "Yet I believe I know you quite well, my dear sir. We do seem to have cause to be naked together on this occasion."

Mael opened his eyes to see hers sparkling with life in a face made rosy by a blush. The rain had washed away the blood from her skin, and when she took a breath it sounded deep and effortless.

"You live," he managed to say. He wanted to roar with joy, but then he saw the confusion in her eyes. Did she remember him, or had she gone back to the lady she'd been in the maze? "Do you ken me, lass?"

She inspected his face leisurely. "Yes, I do. You're Mael mag Raith." Her lips curved. "The man I love."

He cradled her face in return, and kissed her from her mouth to her brow and back again. "Thank the Gods. They brought you back to me."

"So it would seem. Why are we sitting in this tower?" Her gaze shifted up. "And why does it look like it's exploded around us?"

"Sorry to interrupt." A hand extended through a gap in the stones, and held out Mael's tartan along with another he didn't recognize. "Could you maybe put these on and come out of there before my *head* explodes?"

The strain in Jenna's voice had Mael helping Rosealise up to wrap her in his tartan. He then draped himself in the other before guiding her through the gap in the tower wall and into the passage that lead to his chamber. The floor, now covered in new timber, had been strewn with fresh, sweet-scented herbs. Overhead a new thatched ceiling stretched.

Jenna, whose dark hair had been cropped close to her scalp, stood staring back at him. She wore a short gown made from a tartan that resembled Domnall's, only much faded.

"Where on earth have you two been?" she

demanded.

Mael frowned. "In the tower, as you ken. Why did you cut off your hair?"

"I burned off most of it trying to find you. By the way, if you ever need me to walk through stone walls, five is now my hard limit." She walked a short distance away from them, let out a loud whistle, and then returned. "Before the tower, where were you?"

Rosealise shrugged and grimaced up at him. "I remember taking blankets to the buttery last night."

"I went there to look in on you. 'Tis all I remember." He regarded Jenna, amazed to see tears in her eyes. "We didnae mean to worry you, my lady. Did we spring another trap?"

"A trap?" She laughed, shook her head, and pressed the heels of her palms against her eyes before dropping them. "I don't know what happened, but you both disappeared without a trace, and it wasn't last night."

"'Twas three months past," Domnall said as he came to stand beside his wife. "'Tis the middle of summer now, Mael."

Last night for him had been a change of seasons for his clan. Mael glanced back at the tower. "Mayhap you shouldnae go in there again."

"Forget the damn tower." Jenna blinked hard and swiped at her eyes. "We thought you were dead. I even prayed to your lousy Gods. Out loud, where everyone could hear me."

"I believe I was deceased, just a moment ago." Rosealise glanced down and moved aside a fold of Mael's tartan to expose her thigh. The Sluath brand on it had turned golden. "Dun Chaill works its magic again."

Broden came in behind Domnall, stumbled and nearly fell on his face. Edane helped him up as he stared, slack-jawed. To Mael both looked darker and leaner, and the archer had taken to wearing his hair in a single braid. Kiaran was the last to arrive, wearing a smith's heavy leather apron and sporting on his shoulder a fledgling kestrel.

"By the Gods," the falconer said, paling. "Jenna, you must pray for me."

The chieftain's wife uttered a tearful sob as she came and embraced Rosealise, and Domnall did the same to Mael. Then the rest of the hunters demanded the same, with more thanks to the Gods for their blessings.

Chapter Forty

ONCE THEY HAD borrowed
suitable garments, Mael escorted
his lady out to the great hall,
which now contained more furnishings, better
ceilings, and iron grates guarding the fireplaces. That so much work had been accomplished made it evident that the Mag Raith
had not spent their time in mourning, but
Mael glimpsed the changes pain had wrought
in his brothers and sister as well. They all
seemed quieter and yet closer, with the most
marked change in Broden and Edane, who
chided each other as siblings instead of rivals.

"We've done much to the keepe since you
vanished," Domnall said. "We kept your

chamber as 'twas, Seneschal, but we use the buttery for storage of milk, cream, and eggs."

The Englishwoman grinned. "I don't mind sharing with Mael."

Mael folded his hand over hers. "You're trading for dairy now?"

"We discovered Wachvale abandoned at the start of summer," the chieftain said. "They burned the dwellings and took everything of value, so 'twas likely plague. We brought the livestock left behind here to tend them, so we keep cows, sheep, pigs, and even some chickens."

"I've rebuilt the castle's forge," Kiaran said, and stroked the tiny head of the fledgling. "Dive hatched another brood, so we've now nine hunters. They dinnae care for the chickens."

"You look well, my lady," Edane said to Rosealise. "I see no sign of your affliction."

"I believe I'm cured, sir." She touched the base of her throat. "I feel exactly as I did before I fell ill." She breathed in and out deeply, as if to prove it.

"You're immortal now," Jenna told her. "I

should know, I've got the matching ink in gold. Something transformed you."

"Dun Chaill," Broden put in. "Just as it did you, my lady."

The archer shook his head. "They came back naked."

Mael understood his meaning, and put his arm around Rosealise. "You reckon that we returned from the underworld."

"With no memory of the place, as before." Edane gave his lady a sympathetic look. "At least you yet remember your time at Dun Chaill, and among the Mag Raith."

"I do recall who I was in my time," Rosealise told him. "A very lonely woman facing a slow, terrible decline. I had only my work, and even that was stolen from me."

"I take it you're not anxious to go back?" Jenna asked.

"I've been given a second chance to live and be with a man I adore." Rosealise looked around at them. "I hope, too, to be a part of this clan, as you've become like my family. There is no place I'd rather be than here and now."

"You'll have to wed me," Mael told her

sternly. "'Tis the only manner in which you may become Mag Raith."

"Well, except for how we awoke in the enchanted forest and–" Kiaran winced as Broden slapped the back of his head. "I'm mistaken. 'Tis as Mael says."

Rosealise smiled. "I accept your offer, sir, but for love, not your name."

"In my time women can keep our own surnames, you know," Jenna said, and chuckled as Domnall glared at her. "But I like Mag Raith, too."

"So 'tis settled." Mael stood, and with his lady's hand in his fist held out his arm. "Mag Raith *gu bràth.*"

His brothers and sister made a wheel of their arms, holding their fists together at the center.

Domnall covered their fists with his hand. "Mag Raith *gu bràth.*"

Sneak Peek

Edane (Immortal Highlander, Clan Mag Raith Book 3)

Excerpt

CHAPTER ONE

A FINE MIST of rain greeted Edane mag Raith as he led his restless chestnut gelding out of the stable. He flipped his tartan over the quiver and bow at his shoulder to keep both dry. The storm rushed over Dun Chaill in a vast river of gray cloud, parting now and then to allow brief flashes of daylight. They came from the sun, now as a golden bauble surfacing and submerging in the roiling tempest.

Aye. He felt the storm reaching inside him, stirring the change that came only with the wind and rain. *Take me with you.*

Domnall mag Raith came to join him, and surveyed the skies with his shrewd verdant eyes. Tall, broad and heavily muscled, the chieftain dwarfed all but one of his clan.

"I'd ride with you," Domnall said, "but I vowed to Jenna I'd finish the bath chamber today."

"'Tis a patrol of the boundary. Likely the Gods shall but give me and the nag a good wash." Edane swung up onto the gelding, and scanned the storm once more before regarding the chieftain. "Yet if they drop a naked lass in my lap, I'll be longer away."

Domnall grinned and stepped back. "Then I bid you fair hunting, Brother."

The gelding went still as Edane let the storm transform him. Each time he had made the change he imagined he'd feel accustomed to it, but the electric thrill of becoming lighter than air still sizzled through his veins. Brilliant light engulfed him as he touched his heels to the horse's sides, and his mount surged forward. A moment later the gelding's hooves left the ground as they soared up into the clouds.

Edane and the other Mag Raith had quickly learned that their ability to fly came only with a storm. During their first ascent, while battling the Sluath, they had been astounded to discover they could fight their enemy in the air. The winged underworld demons that had long ago enslaved the five hunters had apparently given them the ability, along with other bewildering alterations. The Mag Raith no longer aged or grew sick, and even the gravest wounds they sustained healed rapidly. Each hunter also had a particular power beyond that of an ordinary mortal. How and why the demons had bestowed such gifts remained a mystery, for the Sluath had also stripped the hunters of their memories.

Edane still resented many things the Sluath had done to him and his brothers, but not this. Flying through the lashing rain and howling wind made him feel as he did with a bow in his hands: strong and sure.

Now looking down on the sprawling walls

and towers of Dun Chaill, a sense of accomplishment added to Edane's elation. Left to rot for centuries, the castle had been in ruins when the Mag Raith had arrived to claim it. After the many months he and his clan had spent rebuilding and restoring the keepe, it was beginning to look more like a proper stronghold.

The feel of nearby magic sparkled against his flesh and drew Edane's attention back to the air before him, where he could see the shimmer of the looming spell boundary. He didn't know who had placed the protective enchantment around Dun Chaill and the surrounding forests, but the ancient spell caster had been very powerful. The ward had protected the ruins so closely that not even the smallest insects could cross the spell barrier.

But the Sluath may.

He remembered the lone scout that had attacked the stronghold during another storm. Domnall had slain the demon before it could summon the rest of its infernal horde, but the suddenness of the attack had prompted the chieftain to begin storm patrols.

The mist below Edane parted, and he

frowned as he spotted a pale figure running through the tall grasses of the glen. The only mortals near Dun Chaill had burned and abandoned their village in the spring after what Domnall surmised was an outbreak of plague. This one appeared to be a lad, perhaps left behind to die but now recovered.

His gaze shifted to the flashing light in the clouds behind the boy, from which a Sluath demon descended. Since the demons preyed on mortals left alone and vulnerable, his pursuit could mean only one fate for the lad.

As Edane urged his mount to descend, he reached back to fling aside his tartan as he drew an iron-tipped arrow from his quiver, even as he let his bow slide down into his fist.

"You'll no' steal this one, you fack."

#

If the gorgeous goon with the wings grabbed her, Nellie Quinn knew she'd be cut down like cheap hooch. She'd figured that out the minute she'd eyeballed him swooping in from the clouds, all icy claws and teeth.

"Rebel slut," the goon had hissed. "You'll make a fine prize for our prince."

Whatever big cheese he worked for, Nellie knew he was some kind of button man, so she ran. Now a Robin Hood riding the sky on a horse was coming at her from the other direction, a bow in his hand.

"Oh, swell."

She swerved away, ducking as she did. She heard a whistle and glanced back to see Robin clip the goon with three arrows, one after another, so fast she only saw them hit.

The goon screeched and nearly fell to the ground. Black stuff splashed from his wings as he flapped and lunged back up to disappear into the clouds. Nellie promptly tripped and fell, pain streaking up from her ankle as she flopped into a puddle.

I'm done running.

She rolled over and let the rain wash the mud from her face. The rest of her got a good, cool dousing, too, which was when she realized she was in the altogether. She pushed herself up on her elbows to be sure, and saw Robin Hood running toward her.

Nellie should have tried to crawl off, but

she was too busy enjoying the show. Golly, but he was handsome. Wet scarlet hair poured around a Valentino face. He had eyes so blue they should have been July sky. All that long, keen body made her hands itch to pet him. The only thing she didn't like were the weird black tattoos on his right arm. Something about them made her want to spit.

He can cover them up, Nellie thought, enchanted.

"Lad, arenae you—"

As he got close, he stopped and stared at her bare peaches and kitty.

Not that she had much fruit or fur to show, she thought, and then chuckled with relief. She had what she had, and the goon didn't have her, and that was jake, all because of Robin.

"Not a fella," she said. To show she still had some manners, she held out her hand. "Nellie Quinn. Thanks for drilling that goon. Thought for a minute there I was headed for the big sleep."

"My name's Edane mag Raith." Rather than shake, he tugged the wet green and black blanket from his shoulders and knelt down to cover her with it.

Delighted to have him so close, Nellie curled a hand around his neck, and tugged him forward to give him a quick kiss. He tasted like rain and man, and he smelled even better, so she went back for another, longer try. Oh, what she'd give for a room and a bed and all the time in the world with Edane. He kept his eyes open like hers, but after a bit she realized he wasn't kissing her back.

No point getting stuck on a fella who didn't want her. With a sigh she broke it off.

"Why did you that?" he asked, his breath caressing her lips.

"You saved me." She traced a finger across his pretty mouth. He sure did talk funny, but he was just too sheik for her not to crush on. "So, you got a squeeze back at your joint, or can a girl hope?"

He blinked. "The demon didnae chase you from Wachvale."

"Don't know. I came to, saw the flash and claws, and heard him say something about a prize and a prince. I skedaddled." Strange things flashed through her mind as she wrapped his drippy plaid around her and sat up. "Feeling a bit out on the roof here, Danny. Give me a hand up?"

"No' Danny," he said. "Edane."

"Right." Boy, was he a stickler. As soon as Edane took hold of her, the images faded. Instead Nellie felt something like a hot kiss on the back of her neck, and swiped at it. "Hey, that smarts." She traced the heated marks with her fingertips. "Like something burned me."

Edane stepped behind her, removed her hand, and then made a funny sound. A moment later he came around again, and looked at his arm before he met her gaze.

"You're marked by the Sluath."

"Yeah, sure." She smiled. "What's a Sluath?"

• • • • •

Buy *Edane (Immortal Highlander, Clan Mag Raith Book 3)*

MORE BOOKS BY HH

For a complete, up-to-date book list, visit
HazelHunter.com/books.

Get notifications of new releases and special
promotions by joining my newsletter!

Glossary

Here are some brief definitions to help you navigate the medieval world of the Clan Mag Raith series.

aquila: Latin for "eagle", the standard of a Roman legion

aulden: medieval slang for "archaic"

bairn: child

Banbury tale: Victorian slang for a nonsensical story

bannock: a round, flat loaf of unleavened Scottish bread

bloodwort: alternate name for yarrow

bloomers: Victorian word for "trousers"

blue-stocking: Victorian slang for "intellectual"

boak: Scottish slang for "vomit"

borage: alternate name for starflower (Borago officinalis)

broch: an ancient round hollow-walled structure found only in Scotland

burraidh: Scots Gaelic for "bully"

cac: Scots gaelic for "shit"

chebs: Scottish slang for "breasts"

conclave: druid ruling body

Cornovii: name by which two, or three, tribes were known in Roman Britain

cossetted: cared for in an overindulgent way

cottar: an agricultural worker or tenant given lodgings in return for work

Cuingealach: Scots Gaelic for "the narrow pass"

curate: a member of the clergy engaged as an assistant to a vicar, rector, or parish priest

deadfall trap: a type of trap fashioned to drop a heavy weight on the prey

deamhan (plural: *deamhanan*): Scots Gaelic for demon

dolabra: Latin for "pickaxe"

don't take any wooden nickels: early 20th century American slang for "don't do something stupid"

doss: leaves, moss, and other detritus covering

the ground dru-wid: Proto Celtic word; an early form of "druid"

drystane: a construction of stacked stone or rock that is not mortared together

dunnage: Victorian slang for "clothing"

fash: feel upset or worried

fizzing: Victorian slang for "first-rate" or "excellent"

floorer: Victorian slang for "knocking someone down"

flummery: a custard-like Welsh dessert made from milk, beaten eggs and fruit

footman: a liveried servant whose duties include admitting visitors and waiting at table

frittata: Italian egg dish similar to a crustless quiche

give the sack: English slang for "firing someone from their job"

gladii: Latin plural of *gladius* or "sword"

glock: Victorian slang for "half-wit"

gongoozler: Victorian slang for "an idle, dawdling person"

goof: early 20th century American slang for "a man in love"

grice: a breed of swine found in the Highlands and Islands of Scotland and in Ireland groat: a type of medieval silver coin worth approximately four pence

gu bràth: Scots Gaelic for forever, or until Judgment

hold your wheesht: Scottish slang term for "maintaining silence and calm"

hoor: medieval slang for "whore", "prostitute"

Hussar: member of the light cavalry

in the scud: Scottish slang for "naked"

jem: Medieval Scots slang for a person prized for beauty and excellence, a "gem"

jess: a short leather strap that is fastened around each leg of a hawk

kirk: Scottish slang for "church"

*kithan:*Medieval Scots term for a "demon"

knacker: Victorian slang for "an old, useless horse"

laudanum: a tincture of opium

luaidh: Scots Gaelic for "loved one" or "darling"

maister: medieval slang for "master" or "leader"

make a stuffed bird laugh: Victorian slang phrase for something that is "preposterous or contemptible"

màthair: Scots Gaelic for "mother"

nag: slang for horse

naught-man: an unearthly creature that only looks like a man

nock: the slotted end of an arrow that holds it in place on the bowstring

panay: alternate name for self-heal (*Prunella vulgaris*)

pantaloons: Victorian word for "trousers"

parti: the ideas or plans influencing an architect's design

peignoir: Victorian-era woman's garment similar to a "negligee or a light dressing gown"

peridot: a green semi-precious mineral, a variety of olivine

plumbata: lead-weighted throwing dart used by the Romans

pomatum: greasy, waxy, or water-based substance used to style hair

quern: a primitive hand mill for grinding grain made of two stones

rooing: removing sheep's loose fleece by hand-pulling

sica: a long curved dagger

skeg: Scots Gaelic for "demon"

stand hunt: to watch for prey from a blind or place of concealment stele: an upright pillar bearing inscriptions

stockman: a person who looks after livestock

strewing: plants scattered on the floor as fragrance, insecticide, and disinfectant

tapachd: Scots Gaelic for "an ability of confident character not to be afraid or easily intimidated"

taverit: Scottish slang for "worn out, exhausted"

tear bottle: Used in the Victorian revival of the ancient custom of catching tears of mourning in a small vial with a loose stopper. When the bottled tears evaporated, the period of mourning was considered over.

trigging: in stonework, using wedge pieces to secure a construct

trodge: Scottish slang for "trudge"

valise: a small traveling bag or suitcase

woundwort: alternate name for wound healer (*Anthyllis vulneraria*)

Pronunciation Guide

A selection of the more challenging words in the Immortal Highlander, Clan Mag Raith series.

Aklen: ACK-lin
aquila: uh-KEE-lah
Bacchanalian: back-NIL-ee-ahn
bannock: BAN-ick
boak: BOWK
Broden mag Raith: BRO-din MAG RAYTH
burraidh: BURR-ee
cac: kak
Carac: CARE-ick
Clamhan: CLEM-en
Clarinda Gowdon: kler-IN-dah GOW-don
Cornovii: core-KNOW-vee-eye

Cuingealach: kwin-GILL-ock

Cul: CULL

Danar: dah-NAH

Darro: DAR-oh

deamhan: DEE-man

dolabra: dohl-AH-brah

Domnall mag Raith: DOM-nall
MAG RAYTH

Dun Chaill: DOON CHAYLE

Eara: EER-ah

Edane mag Raith: eh-DAYN MAG RAYTH

Fargas: FAR-gus

Fiana: FEYE-eh-nah

Fraser: FRAY-zir

Frew: FREE

frittata: free-TAH-tah

Galan Aedth: gal-AHN EEDTH

gladii: GLAHD-ee-ee

groat: GROWT

gu bràth: GOO BRATH

Hal Maxwell: HOWL MACK-swell

Hussar: hoo-ZAHR

Iolar: EYE-el-er

Jaeg: YEGG

jem: GEM

Jenna Cameron: JEHN-nah CAM-er-ahn

Kiaran mag Raith: KEER-ahn MAG RAYTH
kithan: KEY-tin
laudanum: LAH-deh-num
luaidh: LOO-ee
Lyle Gordon: lie-EL GORE-din
Mael mag Raith: MAIL MAG RAYTH
maister: MAY-ster
marster: MAR-stir
Mary Gowdon: MARE-ee GOW-don
máthair: muh-THERE
Meirneal: MEER-nee-el
Nectan: NECK-tin
parti: PAR-tee
peignoir: pen-WAH
plumbata: PLOOM-bah-tah
pomatum: pah-MADE-uhm
quern: KWERN
Rodney Percell: RAHD-knee purr-SELL
Rosealise Dashlock: roh-see-AH-less
DASH-lock
Seabhag: SHAH-vock
sica: SEE-kah
Sileas: SIGH-lee-ess
skeg: SKEHG
Sluath: SLEW-ahth
tapachd: TAH-peed

taverit: tah-VAIR-eet
tisane: TEE-zahn
trodge: TRAHJ
valise: vuh-LEES
Wachvale: WATCH-veil
wheesht: WEESHT

Dedication

For Mr. H.

Copyright